I0672928

ISBN: 069270163X

ISBN-13: 978-0692701638

Finding Alana

Meg Farrell

DEDICATION

For my Mama

I love you, and still miss you every day.

ACKNOWLEDGEMENTS

My tribe—Amy, Paulette, Tara, and J-Vo: Thank you for retreats, wine, bong-bong, tattoos, chocolate, and endless laughter.

The Shady Ladies – Thank you for allowing me to be me, and loving me anyway.

Cover design: Cover Me Darling

http://www.covermedarling.com

Editor: Victoria Miller

http://www.victoriamillerartist.com

FROM THE AUTHOR

This book is _loosely_ based on a true story. It contains episodes of domestic violence which made it very difficult for me to write. I've never experienced domestic violence first-hand, but my friends and family have.

Get help if you or anyone you know is struggling with domestic violence. Lives depends on it.

For help with domestic violence:

Visit: www.thehotline.org

or

Call: 1-800-799-7233 (SAFE)

TABLE OF CONTENTS

1 - Death

Oh, God! I suck in a quick deep breath. My chest aches as it heaves, and my head is spinning. I feel nauseated as I rub at the headache behind my eyes. Oh, my God! Pain crawls through my body. Taking a mental assessment, I note that everything hurts. Something large and heavy hit me. For some reason, I can't get my head around it. What was I doing? I run my hand down to my stomach because it's burning like I'm on fire. My hand comes away sticky and wet. Oh, God!

Struggling to sit up, I try to open my eyes. There are light trails keeping me from seeing clearly, but I can tell it's blood. My hand is covered in it. Blinking over and over, I try to clear my eyes, and I see it. My stomach is also covered in blood. Recollection floods my mind—the fight. We had a huge fight. Oh, God! He tore through me. He hit me so hard I flew into the bookcase and it shattered against the wall. Then there was the noise. It was loud and thundering. It echoes in my mind. At that moment, I remember... I've been shot.

As the realization moves on, tears well in my eyes, fear fills every fiber of my being, and my breathing stutters. I test my legs to see if they'll move. My knees protest, but give way to movement. I kick at a pile of rubble, and try to make room to get up. A low grumble comes from beside me and I freeze.

Cautiously, I look around, and see my husband is asleep on the couch. I can tell by his snore that he's sleeping off his drunk. The empties piled on the coffee table confirm my suspicions. As silently as possible, I pull myself up gingerly, and begin to move toward the back of the house. I hold the wall for support and grab my purse off our dresser. There's no time to take anything else. Mentally, I begin thanking God that Ethan is at my sister's, and I'm not dead.

Tears are spilling down my cheeks, but I try to remain quiet as I make my way to the door. I don't even close it behind me because it would make too much noise. I need to get away without waking him. I stumble down the steps of our trailer, trying to think of a plan. I start for the car, but then I think of the noise the engine would make. Think, think, think. I look around.

We don't have any close neighbors, and the car is definitely not an option. My only choice is the woods. If I can just make it through the woods, the road is on the other side, and I can hitch a ride to the hospital. I start praying there will be somebody out tonight. That old road never has much traffic. It would be a miracle if there was someone. I sling my purse over my head so it hangs across my body, and then I start for the woods.

Survival mode must've killed the pain as I find my aching body begins to move faster the closer I get to the woods. I trip several times crossing through, but keep going. That's all I can do is keep working my way through the woods. I have to make it. He'll kill me if he catches me.

Exhausted, and determined to survive, I stumble out on to the road. Headlights are coming toward me as I stand captivated, frozen in place. A large truck just misses me as the tires squeal. This is my chance. Somehow I manage to get my legs moving and I run toward the sound of the truck as fast as my body will let me. A man jumps out of the truck and is running toward me.

He's yelling, but I don't hear him. Ignoring him, I run past him to the passenger side of his truck and climb inside.

He follows me and rips the door open. "What are you doing?"

I swallow hard. "Please help me." I reach out and grab him with my right hand as my left protects the injury in my stomach. "I need help." It's all I can mutter.

He must notice the blood because the next thing I know he's lifting my shirt to look at the wound. When he sees it, all he says is, "Oh, my God. Hang on!"

He climbs in on his side of the truck and the tires scream once more. I collapse deeper into the seat as the adrenaline ebbs, and exhaustion drags me into sleep.

৪৩৪৩৪৩৪৩৪৩৪৩

The nightmare never changes. I'm dying. Bleeding to death on the floor of the trailer I shared with my husband. Cold sweat dots my brow as I sit up and throw the covers off. My breathing is always erratic as I try to calm down and bring my brain back into the present. *I'm okay. I'm okay. He can't hurt me.* I repeat the mantra to myself.

Finally, I feel calm enough to start my day. I finish kicking the covers all the way off and put my feet on the icy, hard-wood floor. It must be below freezing outside. My room stays colder than the rest of the house, but this shit is ridiculous.

I start the shower to warm up, and try to talk myself into going to pee. I know the toilet seat is going to be freezing, and I'm right. As soon as I sit, I let out a squeal because I feel like I've just sat on a block of ice.

"Cold, huh?"

I look up to see my roommate, Kate, standing in the bathroom doorway. She's smirking and holding a cup of coffee.

I groan. "Dammit, Kate! Would it kill you to give me a little privacy?"

She laughs, "Whatever, Alana. We have the same bits and pieces. Do you want breakfast?"

Wiping, I pull my sweatpants back in place. "No. Thanks anyway. I'm going to shower and head into work a little early today."

Shock passes over her face. "You hate that place. What has you acting like an overachiever all of a sudden?" Her dark eyes challenge me.

"Remember me telling you about my friend Rhae? The girl whose husband died? Well, she quit last year, and they've just now decided to fill the spot. I applied, and I'm interviewing today. I want some time to do a little prep."

Her smile is radiant. "Oh, girl! I'm so happy for you! Think you'll like it better if you report to someone other than the Dragon Lady?"

"That's my thought. Now, get out of here. I need to shower. We'll talk later." I push at her as she nearly refuses to leave. She knows I won't get naked in front of her. She's always pushing me on this, though. Kate is an exhibitionist and will literally walk around naked in front of anyone. Anyone.

Her body is killer. She should be proud of it. Her skin is a lovely dark brown, and her eyes are even darker. She changes her hair every other day or so. I never know if I should expect to see her with braids or in a big halo around her head. I know it will always be just gorgeous! I've told her a hundred times that she should be modeling.

We've shared the house her grandmother left her for a couple of years. The house is about a hundred years old. Pretty typical for midtown Memphis. My suite is an addition that was built in the sixties. There are a number of updates I think would make it stellar, of which, insulation in the walls is a priority.

Memphis doesn't get a deep freeze like some parts of the country, but when the temperature drops, you can feel it in your bones. We only get one or two snow days a year. On average we just get ice. My room feels like a meat locker through most of the winter. Maybe, if I stay another year, Kate will let me help her finance the work to update it. The drafts can't be good for the electric bill, and it's not safe to keep a space heater on all the time.

I jump in the shower and start preparing for the day ahead of me. I focus on the job description for the position I applied for. The requirements are in my mind like a photographic memory. I don't have a photographic memory, but it's so important I memorized them. The only obstacle could be my education. I didn't go to a big, fancy, college for a bachelor's degree. I had to settle for a community college, which I finished recently. Considering what I've lived through, it's a miracle I got this far.

Fact is, I'm twenty-eight, so my lack of education looks like lack of motivation. How can I tell a potential manager my story? I don't generally advertise it. The only people who know that story in its entirety is my ex-husband, the women's shelter, and the sweet lady who helped fund my college. I will be forever grateful to Cade's grandmother, Irma.

Cade is Rhae's boyfriend. He was living with his grandmother, taking care of his grandfather, down the street from Rhae. It was a wacky chance thing when they met. After they decided to relocate to New Orleans together, they had a moving day party. That's when I got to meet Irma. Boy, is she a fireball!

Small package, and dynamite when she opens her mouth. Like most good, old southern women, she is in charge of all things. Her accent is a bit more Cajun than plain old southern. Of course, she is from Louisiana, though she's quick to tell you she ain't from New Orleans.

She's a petite woman with silver, curly hair, which she keeps knotted in a bun on the top of her head, and she smiles as if she knows everything about you without asking. That's what happened to me. I smile when I think about the conversation she and I had the day I told her about my past.

ᔓᓂᔓᓂᔓᓂᔓᓂᔓᓂᔓᓂᔓ

Irma asked me to walk her home. Being as small and frail as she seemed, I agreed. When we got to her house, she asked me to sit on the porch swing for a spell. She joined me, and then she began.

"Girl, there's all kinds of trouble following you."

Her proclamation surprised me. I must have been an open book to her because I could feel the blood drain from my face only to be replaced by the heat of a blush. All I could do was nod in response.

Irma smiled at me. "Well, I'm glad you ain't trying ta deny it, sweetpea. Let's go see what we can see about this." She stood and led me through her house to the back room. "Now, listen here, what we talk about in this room is only for us. You don't need to share it with nobody if you don't want to. Understand me?"

Still in shock, and a little scared about where this would go, all I could do was nod. Part of me thought this was either one of those gypsy things you grow up seeing on TV, or this lady was out of her mind.

"Good. Now, you be totally honest with me. Tell me about you."

I had to think about where to start. Remembering she'd demanded honesty, and I had her confidentiality, I decided I need to tell her everything. When I finished, she was crying. I felt like total shit making this old lady, whom I'd just met, cry like that.

Irma held my hands, turning my palms to where she could get a good look at them. She mumbled something so low that I couldn't quiet hear what she said. When she looked at me again, there was something new in her face. Determination. Then she laid out the plan. She was taking me as her own. She explained that she wouldn't tell me where I'd end up, but she had seen it. She saw that she needed to help me in any way she could. To her, that meant helping me finish college.

Irma is as important to me as my own grandmother once was. She helped set me on the path so my life could mean something.
Here lately, she's getting down more and more every day. I keep Cade and Rhae informed of her status. I think it's just old age. She refuses to go to the doctor, so I can't say for sure what's wrong with her. I do my best to influence her to see a doctor, but she keeps saying she has seen what's coming for her and when. Irma doesn't want any of us to worry. It scares me, but Cade says that I have to trust her. It goes against all my better judgment, but I know he's right. I've trusted her this far, and she's never been wrong.

2 - Meetings

I arrive to work about an hour ahead of my normal start time. The office is a ghost town. The lights aren't even on yet. I settle into my desk and start reading my resume again and check my calendar. I have several administrative things to do today. My interviews are interspersed between other obligations, and I don't know why I always volunteer for so much. My current job is the lowest rung of the proverbial ladder. Sometimes I think it's one step below entry level.

It's not about where you are; it's about where you're going. Irma's reminder echoes in my mind whenever I think about her words. Her reminders sometimes feel like admonitions for a lack of faith. I look down at the tattoo on my wrist. It's a beautiful script, which reads, "Actually, I can."

Six months ago, when I was having a really low day, I ran across this phrase and knew I needed it as a tattoo. It was such a bad day that I considered quitting school. The only thing that kept me going was knowing how quitting would hurt Irma. It was a day when I was thinking of Ethan, my son.

Ethan was only three years old when I had to run for my life. His tiny face is always in the back of my mind. I don't have any pictures of him, and I haven't been able to see him in five years. I had become very good about keeping my thoughts off of him. He lived only in a tiny compartment of my mind that I accessed when I was alone.

On that particular day, I met another Ethan. He was some guy in my civics class. We were doing introductions as it was the first day of the semester. When he said his name, I jumped and turned to look at him. He had light brown hair and green eyes. The same green as my own. The same as my Ethan.

It was a silly, coincidental moment. It wasn't enough to really call it coincidental. I think Ethan had been on my mind lately, and it was the tiny straw that destroyed the wall holding back all of those pent up emotions. I ran from class, and hid in my car. It was a hell of a thing to explain to the teacher when I returned to class on the following Thursday.

How do you tell your teacher that the guy three rows back reminded you of the son you haven't seen in five years? You don't. You claim lady problems.

That weekend, after I told the negative demon in my head—who tells me all that I can't do—to shut up, I drove to see my friend Allie. She's a tattoo artist. At first, she gave me shit about the phrase, but she drew it up anyway. She did a beautiful job. It wasn't as painful as I thought it might be, and the script is what I need on days like this.

It's a reminder that no matter what shit I've been through, I can do anything I set my mind to do. Right now, I just want to get through these interviews.

I start working through my emails, and printing reports that the Dragon Lady will be asking for. If I can do what she wants before she asks, my life goes a lot smoother. Naturally, the printer shared by the entire cube farm jams. I know because I can hear that dinosaur grinding and squealing. I start praying as I walk over to the beast.

Last time this happened, I was less than successful in fixing it. I sincerely detest calling for the systems guy to come up and look at it. Invariably, they make me feel like an idiot for needing assistance.

First, I read the display to see if it points out on the diagram where the paper is stuck. It does, but it says there are four potential locations for the jam. *Oh* boy. I set about opening all the little doors and turning all the little wheels. I have to be careful because the damn fuser is putting off so much heat that I'm scared to burn myself.

Pulling pages out as I find them, I soon have a stack of torn, crumpled, remnants. I look a little deeper to see a tiny piece hanging behind a pressure plate. After studying the diagrams and arrows printed inside the printer cavity, I see I should lift this green lever that looks to release the plate in question.

I can't seem to move the piece-of-shit lever. So I step back and position my legs to help me. I'm also careful to keep my distance from the machine as my hands look like I've been grease-monkeying on cars, not fixing a printer. I really don't have the money to start replacing my wardrobe due to toner mishaps.

Taking a solid grip on the lever from hell, I bend my knees to leverage some strength from my legs. As I begin to lift, I feel the sudden success of something letting go. I'm just about to fist pump to celebrate my victory over the printer, when I look down to see the lever in my hand—no longer attached to the printer.

"Motherfucker!" I say in frustration, a little louder than I intend. Suddenly, I hear someone behind me clear their throat. *Oh, for fuck's sake.* I take a deep breath, bracing myself to see who I've offended. Slowly, I turn and plaster on a sheepish smile. Standing behind me isn't someone I know. He's grinning from ear to ear like a Cheshire cat.

"Well, it looks like you're going to have some trouble with that printer," he observes.

I nod. "Yeah, guess I got a little carried away with removing a paper jam."

He lets out a noise that can best be described as a cough-laugh-snort. "Ya think? You broke the damn lever off. That's an expensive part to replace," he points out, ever so helpfully.

Irritation courses through me as heat floods my face. I'm embarrassed and pissed. Embarrassed I was dumb enough to bust the lever of the printer, and pissed he would make fun of me. I have no idea who he is or where he's come from. *Who does asshole think he is?* I open my mouth to argue with him and let him know what an ass I think he is, but I never get the chance. He cuts me off.

"Sorry. I couldn't help it. I had to mess with you. You were just so into fixing that paper jam," he says, laughing.

I'm not laughing. My eyebrows pull in as I frown and let my resting bitch face slide into place. "How long were you behind me?"

"Long enough." He winks, and I want to punch him in those luscious brown eyes. "I'm Justin." He holds his hand out for an introductory shake. "I work for Wilson Technical."

I don't shake his hand. I fold my arms over my chest. "And?" I ask. Like I'm supposed to know what Wilson Technical is and why it's important.

All signs of laughter disappear, and his smile fades. "I, uh, I'm here to replace the printer." He ends his sentence with a nod that says, *"Get it?"*

I shake my head to clear it of the agitation swirling around. "Oh. Okay. Well. Carry on, Justin." I roll my eyes and walk away. I head over to my desk to grab my coffee cup. This shit went down way too early this morning. I need a drink—a real drink. Coffee will have to do.

Naturally, the pot is empty, but someone left the machine running at some point. Now that's been sitting all weekend, there is a nasty, thick, black sludge in the bottom of it. I huff as I take the pot to the sink in the break area and start running the water so it can heat up.

As I'm waiting, I place my hands on the edge of the counter, drop my head, and let my shoulders sag. This day is too important, and everything is falling apart. I close my eyes while the water continues to run and practice breathing. *In and Out. In. And out.* I repeat the words in my head to try and regain some focus.

"Water's hot."

I jump and let out a surprised squeak as I clap my hand over my mouth to stifle whatever else might come after it. That's when I see him. Printer guy, Justin. *Really?* "Uh, yeah. Thanks for the observation." I roll my eyes again, and add soap to the sludge-crusted coffee pot to start scrubbing.

Justin clears his throat with a *pay-attention-to-me* sound. I don't look at him. I guess he figures that's permission to keep talking. "Look, we got off on the wrong foot. I didn't mean to laugh at you. I meant it when I said I was sorry."

Still scrubbing, I say, "Yeah, well, you did. So..."

He sighs. "It was funny because you were working so hard on the printer they reported last week and asked us to replace. You clearly didn't know it was already dead." He sounds sincere.

I stop scrubbing, and turn to look at him. He's your average guy. Not remarkably tall, easily six-foot, but I doubt an inch more. His dark brown hair swoops across his face, clearly too long. It's annoying and adorable how he flips it back every now and then. His brown eyes are huge and give the perception of depth. They are...interesting.

The exhaustion from being so worked up about the day, and scrubbing the coffee pot hits me all at once. I lean my back against the wall by the sink, and rest my elbow on the counter. Surrendering. "It's okay," I mutter. "It's not your fault I took it so bad. It's been a shitty start to a very important day. I'm wound up, I guess. Mondays, ya know?" I try to give him a smile, but it feels awkward and fake.

He steps over to the counter I'm leaning against, the corners of his mouth turning up a little bit, "What makes today so important?"

I shrug. "Nothing major to anyone else. I'm interviewing for a promotion I've waited nearly a year for them to open up. I need this to go well."

"That is an important day. And it is pretty major. Sorry I was a part of stressing you out more."

I really smile now because he's kind, and there's an odd peace crawling its way through my veins. Almost as if being in his presence is a stress antidote. "It's not your fault. You couldn't know."

"Would it help if I said you got this?" he asks.

I chuckle as I turn to face him and let go of the last of my animosity. "I'm not sure what that means, or how you would know, but yeah, that helps."

The smile he gives me is megawatt-bright. "Good. You got this! I should go finish my work order." He straightens and starts walking toward the door.

"Thanks," I say in a near whisper.

As he's about to leave the kitchen, he turns back. "Oh, who should I say broke the printer?"

I give him a sarcastic smile. "Alana."

3 - Coincidence

"Wine after work tonight." I text Kate on my way back to my desk.

Her response is nearly instantaneous, and, as usual, emphatic. *"Hell yeah! Only, let's skip wine at home and go to the bar."*

I chuckle and text her back a time to meet at the house. I'm glad I have her. She's been seriously dependable and more supportive than any other random roommate I could've found. She's a blessing.

Work is rote as I finish preparing reports. My manager, Bernice, AKA the Dragon Lady, has decided she wants all reports presented in a color-coded file system. I have an instructional document on how to present reports to her.

It's fucking ridiculous, yet I keep my mouth shut and do as I'm told, playing the get-along game. I need this job, and I need the promotion even more.

Checking my calendar for the millionth time, I note that I have ten minutes until my first interview of four today. Four interviews for a single-step promotion. I won't even be a manager level, yet I need to interview with four people to get there. It's a tad excessive.

I consider my answers to the questions I hate the most: *What is your biggest weakness? What is your five-year plan?* Dude, I so just want to answer: *I have no weaknesses. My five-year plan is to have a job and stay alive.* That won't float, so I polish my professional responses.

I have to convince them I want to be here for the rest of my life. *Go Web Design, Inc.!* I bleed blue and white. Damn it! Maybe I should have worn a company logo shirt. Too late now. I find myself watching the clock as my thoughts ramble.

I remember how Rhae used to look at me when I would chase rabbits. She used to call me a squirrel. The memory puts a smile on my face. *It's time. Get your shit together.* I stand and walk toward the conference room.

The first interview is with the hiring manager, Dee. She is a sweet lady. Her questions are easy. She's very casual and makes me feel comfortable. Surprisingly, she never asks me the dreaded weakness question. Interview number two is another web designer that works for Dee. I guess he's her number one since Rhae left. He's a cocky prick. I have to overlook that to be as personable as possible. *I need this job. I need this job.* I repeat as I do my mental mantras that keep me on the right trick.

I've used mental mantras since, well, since that night. I needed them to keep my feet moving. I'm my own best inspiration and motivation. My mind wanders as I answer the same questions Dee asked.

It's like muscle memory. My answers are consistent, witty, and real. Before I know it, I have his cocky ass laughing. It makes me feel like I might be able to fit-in on Dee's team.

I have a break after the second interview to grab some lunch. It's already much later than I typically go out. My body is exhausted. It's as though I've been running a marathon after these interviews. I think I tense my muscles while I'm in those meetings.

Maybe I'm making this too big a deal in my mind. There has to be a way to relax through the process. What's the worst that could happen? I don't get it? Big deal. I still have my administrative job if that happens.

I decide to lunch alone at the deli two blocks away. As I leave our building and step out onto the sidewalk, the temperature hits me like I've walked into an invisible wall. The wind lifts my hair from my neck and blows it straight back. I fight with the hood of my coat to cover my ears as I silently reprimand myself for not putting the hood up while I was still inside.

Eventually, I tame all the bits of red by tucking them under it. I'm still not really used to being a red-head. I started coloring my hair after I left. Now, I change it every so often to keep it fresh. Well, that's what I tell everyone.

The real reason is I'm not sure if my ex is still looking for me or not. I constantly worry he's going to show up one day. Okay, I don't worry. I'm petrified that will happen. I'm not sure how he would be able to find me.

The women's shelter I lived in for a year had contacts in law enforcement. They helped me apply for a name change, new social security number—a whole new identity. Something I will never be able to repay.

I'm beginning to regret taking lunch alone because being alone affords me nothing but time to dwell on everything. It's very easy for me to get lost in those memories. Every time I start down this road, I feel like a gaping hole punches through my chest. Guilt and pain consume me because I am the worst mother in the history of the world. I saved myself and left my baby there.

The only minor comfort I can give myself is knowing, or thinking, Kent would never lay hands on our boy. Ethan was always supposed to be his greatest achievement. His legacy. He wouldn't abuse him the way he did me. He couldn't.

As I approach the deli, I can see Lucy and Jules sitting at a table near the front window. They catch sight of me and start waving me over to sit with them. I'm so relieved not to be alone that I don't even hesitate. I hug them both, and take a seat at the table.

"Girl! We would have invited you to come with us, but we didn't think you were going out for lunch today," Lucy rambles an explanation.

I smile. "I know you would have. I didn't think I was either. I've had two interviews this morning, and two more after lunch. How's Monday going for you guys?"

We talk a little while and order food. I opt for soup and a salad. My mind drifts a little as the others talk about their day. I'm looking around distracted and see a newly familiar face walk in the door. Justin, the printer guy, comes into the deli. He seems to be scanning the room as if trying to find the people he's meeting. As he moves closer, I stare down at my food, hoping he doesn't notice me. I take a deep breath and decide to reach for my phone to use as a busy disguise. When I take it out of my coat pocket, I drop it on the floor. Heat creeps into my face, and I know I'm blushing. I close my eyes to try and calm myself down.

"Oops, here you go."

I know who it is without looking and know he's holding the phone out to me. I glance up and look right into his eyes. Those dark comforting brown eyes. His all-American, megawatt smile seems out of place with his tattoos and beanie hat. I immediately notice the script on his forearm. It's wide, bold, Old English font. I don't know what it means. Looks like Latin, if I had to guess. I must look confused because he feels the need to explain.

"You, uh, dropped this. Not your day for technology," he muses.

"Yeah. Not my day. Sorry." I shake myself and take the phone. "Thank you. Rescuing me again."

"I don't know about a rescue; I just seem to be where you need me today. Alana, right?"

I nod. "Justin, right?"

"Yeah. Glad you remembered. Has your day gotten any better?"

I smile. "It has. Lunch with my girls makes everything better."

Realization crosses his face, and he reaches up to pull his knit hat off his head. That dark brown hair stands on end. It's the best hat hair I've ever seen. My breath hitches. Justin sets about introducing himself to Lucy and Jules. They are left speechless, which is saying something for this group.

I start wishing Rhae was here. She'd have some odd sarcastic thing to say. When he finishes smiling and shaking hands, he leans closer to me. "See you later."

Before I can help myself, I reach up and smooth down his unruly hair, and say, "Sure thing." It's a habit response, I think. I have no idea if I'll ever see him again. Chances are, since he's assigned to our business account, he'll be in the building more often.

Justin clears his throat, and I realize I'm still patting his hair down. I freeze, and slowly pull my hand back. Rolling my lips in so they disappear, I force myself to avoid eye contact with him and mutter a very small, "Sorry."

"Thanks," he says in a voice just a quiet as my apology. I glance up in time to see him walking away to join his lunch group and catch the small wave he gives me as he goes.

I exhale and I feel like a weight has been lifted. I didn't even realize I was holding my breath. This is new. I haven't thought about any guy like that since...

"Earth to Alana!" Jules says. Lucy is laughing so hard there are tears in her eyes. "Where did you go over there?"

I shake my head. "What are you talking about? I'm right here, dopey."

"Yeah, well, you are totally into him," Jules gloats.

"I'm not. I just met him this morning."

Not letting it go, Jules goes on, "Uh, yeah, so if you aren't into him, then you are feeling motherly toward him? What is up with you fixing his hair?"

I glare, speechless.

Lucy interjects, "What happened this morning?"

"He was an asshole," I answer. "He stood there watching me try and remove a paper jam in that stupid printer. Never said a word, then laughed at me when I snapped a lever off the damn thing."

"Mr. Man doesn't seem like an asshole. Maybe slightly hipster, but not asshole," Jules observes.

Lucy adds, "Yeah, what did he mean he'll see you later? Did you get his number?"

"Settle down. Seriously. You know I don't date. I don't have his number. He's the new account rep for the tech company that handles our outsourced hardware. I think he meant he'll see me around the building. You two are incurable romantics."

Jules shrugs. "We helped Rhae work that out, didn't we?"

I roll my eyes. "No. Rhae did that on her own. Speaking of which, we need to call her later. I miss her something crazy."

When we return to work, I rock the last two interviews. I'm floating through the remainder of the day, and by five-thirty, I'm in the car headed home to meet Kate for a night out. It's a pre-promotion celebration! I'm in the bathroom changing clothes when she gets home, late as usual. If I want her somewhere at six P.M., I tell her five-thirty to be sure she'll be on time.

"Hey, Alana! You ready?" Kate yells as she walks through the front door, slamming it behind her.

"Yeah. Five minutes," I yell back.

"Two minutes," she replies, standing behind me.

Startled, my heart leaps into my throat. "What the fuck, Kate? You know I hate it when you surprise me like that!"

She holds her hands up. "Sorry. How did the interviews go?"

"I rocked that shit. Let's go drink!" I answer as I pull my long-sleeved pink V-neck T-shirt over my head. I had put my jeans and combat boots on before Kate showed up.

"Ready," I say and let Kate lead the way as I follow her out of my room. I grab my jacket and purse right before closing the front door.

We live down the street from our favorite bar. It might be our favorite bar because it's just down the street. Convenience wins when you don't have a designated driver. We walk in and find our usual table empty.

Kate waves at the bartender, Todd, as we head for our favorite table. He waves back at Kate, then throws a, "Hey Alana!" at me. Todd has been after me for a long time, but I'm not interested. He's nice, not bad looking; just not for me. We slide into the booth, sagging into the squishy seat, ready to drink away our day. I don't want to talk about my day, so I let Kate take lead on this conversation.

She's been having problems with a guy at work. I think its sexual harassment, but she's afraid to say anything because the guy has family connections to the owner. It's a bullshit answer. I don't think that is ever okay.

I start mentally planning to help her get my old admin job once they officially promote me. No woman deserves cat calling and random comments about how hot she is at work. No matter how hot she may be, and Kate is very hot. I don't say anything about reporting him anymore. I know she won't, and it upsets her when I say anything about it.

Todd comes over to the table with a couple of beers. Someone starts the jukebox. I much prefer live music to the jukebox. Mainly because there's no telling what people will pick. Kate and I are good friends with the band that usually plays here. As we should be since we hang out here all the time. She actually has an on-and-off thing with the singer. I keep telling her how cliché that is, but Kate is her own person. She really, truly doesn't care if someone is judging her. It's their problem, not hers.

Kate takes a break from her rant about the asshole at work to ask about my day. I shrug her off because I don't want to rehash the whole interview process. It's boring as hell. I take a big drink off my beer, and when I put the bottle down. I simply tell her, "Nothing major happened. Average day in the cube life."

"Just average?" I look up to see Justin standing by our table with a friend I remember from his lunch group. I never even saw them come in the bar.

I'm stunned by the fact he's here, and this is the third time today we have "run into each other." Something starts to feel not-random about it, but I can never tell if it's a real feeling or my paranoia getting the better of me. I narrow my eyes at him before I answer, "Nothing major. Just average."

He laughs, and it is a great laugh. *Oh God*. I decide how much I like that laugh. Something inside me melts. My resolve and suspicions become cloudy. My mind aches as I try to resist the urge, but my body doesn't listen to my mind around him. I find myself smiling. *Fail*. Kate invites them to sit down.

Justin looks at me, before sitting. "Are you okay with us staying?"

He's asking you, dummy. I chastise myself. Stammering, I answer as I start sliding over to make room, "Yeah, sure. Why not?"

Justin slides in beside me while his friend takes a seat next to Kate. Justin introduces his friend, Cameron, to us. Cameron's gaze haven't left Kate's boobs since I noticed the guys standing beside the table. She's eating it up! This is the kind of attention she loves in a social setting.

I steal another look at Justin, and he's pulling that knit hat off his head, tucking into the inner pocket of his seriously worn-out leather jacket. The booth is small and he's close enough to me that I smell the leather of his jacket. He's smoothing his hair, and every move he makes sends more of his smell my way.

It reminds me of my father; an earthy mix of cologne, faint cigarettes, and an old truck. It's intoxicating. Memories spill through my mind, taking me on a quick journey back to my childhood home. I lean toward him, eyes closed, taking a long, deep breath. When I open my eyes and look at him, his bright eyes are smiling down at me.

"Nice, right?"

Busted. I smile sheepishly. "I can't help myself, I love real leather."

He nods his agreement. "It was my Dad's. I stole it in middle school, and I've been wearing it ever since."

"Was the hat your Dad's too?" I ask.

"That? Uh, well, no. That's a gift."

"A gift? From who?" *Please don't say girlfriend.* I suddenly care too much about this answer. It doesn't matter if he has a girlfriend. It's not like I want to date him. *Maybe jump him, but not date.*

He laughs. "It was a gift from my aunt. She knits."

I puzzle it over for a moment and then ask the one question that's been bothering me since he sat down at our table, "So, Justin, are you stalking me?"

His laugh is booming as I, apparently, struck him as completely hilarious. Tears form in the corners of his eyes, and he gasps for air. Looking at me, he seems to be shocked I'm not laughing. His eyes widen before he answers, "What? Stalking? No."

I raise my eyebrow in an expression that tells him I doubt his answer. "Really? Today at work was explainable by the printer. Lunch was easy enough to connect by your proximity to work. But, dude, tonight? Tonight is stalking territory. There's no good explanation for how we have run into each other 'randomly.'" I do air quotes. "Three times in the same day."

His eyebrows pull in as he frowns. "There's a great explanation for all of that." Something occurs to him and his expression changes from frustrated to cocky. "You just fail to see it."

This pisses me off, but I'm going to hold back and give him a chance to explain. "Why don't you explain what I fail to see, then?" I demand as I cut my eyes at him.

The grin that moves from the corner of his mouth to his entire face is entirely too adorable. I need another beer. He starts to answer, but I put my hand on his mouth. "Wait. I need a beer before you try to sell me some bullshit."

"Got it." He jumps up from the booth and goes to the bar. When he settles up with Todd, he has four beers in his hands. He's bought a round for the whole table. Kate and I make eye contact. She winks. I groan.

It's easy to push guys away because most of them are assholes with some motive (read: sex). They are selfish, at least in my experience. The fact that Justin thought of all of us and bought a round is a small clue that he may not be like all the other guys. He doesn't make a big production of passing out the drinks. He just sets them on the table. All but mine. He holds it out to me. "Ultra, right?"

Reluctantly, I give him a small nod as I reach for it. I'm not in the habit of letting guys buy me drinks. Nothing good comes from it; never has. There are expectations behind those gestures. Somehow, I manage to mutter a small, "thank you."

"So, I owe you an explanation," he starts as he settles back into his seat. "Well, it's not stalking. It's been total chance that we have run into each other. I think all things happen for a reason. I don't know if it's God, or the universe, or whatever." He waves his hand in the air dismissively. "Somehow we keep finding each other. That's why I've made it a point to speak to you every time. Whatever the it is, I want to give it a chance to reveal itself."

All I can do is stare at him. *What is he? Where did he come from? He's weird, yet strangely perfect.*

Justin leans toward me and places his mouth next to my ear. "Close your mouth, Alana." I shiver. He chuckles, and pulls back from me slightly. Still close enough that I can feel the warmth of his breath on my cheek, and far enough that we can make eye contact. The parts of me that melted earlier have gone full liquid. This is the feeling I love about being with someone, and it's the feeling I hate. This means I've let my guard down some. I cannot afford to do that. My feet feel numb as realization sinks through me. His eyes on mine are too intense.

I break our eye contact by taking a sip of beer. Cameron grabs his attention. In bar whispers, which are not really whispers, they discuss cancelling their post-bar plans. Something about meeting other friends for dinner.

Kate sends me a quick text while they're talking, *"Holy shit. You met him at work? What's he do there?"*

I text her back, *"Later."*

Her answer is swift, *"Damn right! So, you okay if I take Cameron home tonight?"*

"You've known him like five seconds. What is wrong with you?"

Justin and Cameron are staring at us now. Apparently they can tell we're texting. Kate's look is still questioning, but she shrugs at my text. I simply nod as an answer to her earlier question.

Kate doesn't have strict rules for her sexuality. If she wants something, she goes for it. If she wants to do something, she does it. I love her, and while I see some of her behavior as self-destructive, it's not my place to say anything about who she takes home or sleeps with.

The night wears on and the boys keep buying us beers. Kate and I don't pay for a single drink. We talk and laugh all night. Their stories are incredible. It's a wonder they've survived as long as they have. They are both about to turn thirty. Their birthdays are just weeks apart. They were high school buddies. Cameron always had a car, and Justin always had an idea. They stayed in trouble with law enforcement, school authorities, and landed in juvie several times. Justin settled down when he decided he wanted to go into law enforcement. Cameron followed him into the academy. That's what best friends do. They can't function without each other and going into a dangerous profession meant they were going together.

As I'm listening to their story about the time Cameron accidentally tazed himself, I start opening and closing my mouth. My teeth feel soft. Or maybe I just can't feel them at all. I'm attempting to clack my teeth together to tell for sure, and reach my fingers up to rub my nose. My nose is numb, too. Realization dawns on me; I'm drunk. I start laughing at Cameron's description of flopping on the floor like a fish and taking too much comfort in Justin. His arm is around my shoulder, and I'm leaning against him. In the middle of the story, I'm laughing so hard I can't catch my breath.

Justin sweeps my hair back from my face. "You feeling okay?"

I nod. "Perfect."

"You sure? You keep patting your nose."

"It's numb."

"Ah! The old numb nose. I love that time of night."

Still trying to piece him together, and being drunk, I'm a bit overly blunt, "But you aren't a cop, though."

Justin shakes his head. "Nope. I'm not." He winks.

"But, why?" I ask.

He shakes his head. "That, my dear, is a story for another night. And we'll need many more beers." After a beat of silence, he slaps his palm on the table. "Dance with me," he demands.

"No."

"Please dance with me?" he asks sweetly.

"No. I don't dance," I answer with just a touch of disdain in my voice and screw my face into a frown.

"Make you a deal. You dance with me, one dance, and I'll take you home."

I check my phone for the time. *Shit!* It's after midnight, and I have work tomorrow. I think about his deal. As I'm about to decline for the third time, the music shifts. It's something much sweeter and slower. It's actually one of my favorite songs right now.

The Arctic Monkeys start crooning, but it's the line about a coffee pot that makes me realize who played this song. I gape and then slug him in the arm. He slides out of the booth and reaches his hand out to me.

I smile and take his hand. We don't bother with going to the dance floor. He takes my left hand in his right, and puts his left arm around my waist. The alcohol has my balance off, so I lean into him more than I want to, resting my head on his chest. The way I'm positioned doesn't work for the left hand coupling, so he releases my hand and wraps his right arm around my waist, too. I reach up, winding my arms around his neck.

As we sway, he leans down and whispers in my ear, "I'm glad you ripped that lever off the printer." I let out a very unladylike, embarrassing snort. I turn my face to his neck and take a long sniff as I move my nose from his collar to his ear.

When I reach his ear, I kiss the tender spot right behind his ear lobe, and whisper, "Me too." He reacts by squeezing me a little tighter so I lean back enough to see his face. His expression is unreadable.

I'm shocked by my own behavior, and I'm trying to come up with some kind of excuse or way out of this when he says, "Stay here."

Now, it may be the fact that I'm drunk as shit, but I start to protest. I mean, where am I going? We're beside the table. I turn to say something to Kate and notice we are *not* beside the table. Apparently, our drunk-sway dancing has pulled us to the middle of the bar.

I see Justin with an armload of our jackets and my purse. He shakes hands with Cameron, then kisses Kate on the cheek. When he returns to me, he helps me put my jacket on before putting on his own. Then he tucks my purse under his arm, and takes my hand, pulling me toward the door.

He loads us into a truck. It's an old one that has seen better days. That's part of why he smells like he does. Like my dad and old trucks. When he turns the engine on, the radio comes on automatically. It's blaringly loud. I cover my ears as he fumbles with the knob to turn it down. Finally, he just smacks it until the radio turns off.

"Sorry," he mumbles.

"Wait! Aren't you drunk, too?"

"Nope. I stopped drinking hours ago."

His answer kind of pisses me off, but at the same time, I'm incapable of really complaining.

The silence during the ride is awkward, and the truck is too full of him. I'm starting to feel overwhelmed, so I roll down the window. It's freezing, and I hold my face out into the night as if I'm absorbing the sun on a summer day. Finally, cold enough to break through the haze, I ask, "Where are we going?"

"Your place. I'm taking you home. You've had too much to drink."

I frown. "What if I don't want to go home right now? What about Kate? How do you know where I live?" I'm confused, and my agitation is growing.

"Shhhh. Calm down," he tries to soothe me. "She's fine. She and Cameron are going to our place. Kate told me where you live."

"Why would she go to your place with Cameron?" As soon as the question leaves my lips, I know exactly why she would do that. Then I remember our texts from earlier. I giggle like a little kid, and right before the giggles give way to snorts, "*Ohhhhhhh*, okay. Got it."

The giggles are apparently contagious. Justin's face cracks and he starts laughing, too. There are tears in both of our eyes by the time we pull into my driveway. He comes around to open my door and offers me his hand as I get out. Justin is ever the gentleman by wrapping his arm around me to provide warmth and stability as we take it easy going up the slightly icy steps. I fumble with my key and eventually give up, handing it over to him. "Here! You do this. I can't."

He takes the key and makes quick work of getting us inside. We step into the living room, and Justin seems distracted as he takes in our cozy little place.

Something about the ridiculous laughter, and proximity to him has me feeling not only attracted to him, but anxious to see where this is going. My mind and body are disconnecting. My mind reminds me of all the reasons I don't get involved with anyone. My body is reacting to him. Somewhere deep inside, I remember it could just be the alcohol.

Pondering through all of the reasons and options, I attempt to take my jacket off. Losing my balance, I start to fall. Slightly panicked, I grab for Justin, and catch a handful of shirt as I fall backward onto the sofa. He falls on top of me, and is about to apologize, but I won't let him. I kiss him.

He's surprised, but kisses me back after the surprise passes. His kiss is gentle and is soon growing in intensity becoming possessive. Justin's kiss is hungry. A starved man who's found exactly what he's been looking for. I slide my hands under his jacket and under his shirt to feel his warmth. He jumps and gasps for air.

"Woah! Cold hands!"

"So warm them up," I challenge.

The moment broken, he stands and takes off his jacket. When he's finished, I take his hand and lead him to my bedroom. I sit to untie my combat boots, and he slides his chucks off by the door. Boots unlaced, I fall off the chair as I try to pull the first one off. I'm laughing like an idiot when I see Justin shake his head and kneel in front of me. "Let me do this. You'll hurt yourself."

After the second boot comes off, he stands, helps me up, then takes off his T-shirt. I gape. The man is beautiful. The police academy was good to him. He must work a ton to keep that body.

Noticing I'm frozen, and obviously appreciating his body, he steps closer to me, reaching out a hand to cup my cheek. Using his other hand to cradle my face, he guides my mouth back to his. I breathe in his scent all the way to my core because, for some reason, I can't get enough. He feels... safe. I reach for the button on his jeans, and he reaches for mine. We shimmy out of our jeans and make our way onto my bed, mouths never relenting in their respective exploration of the other.

On the bed, he lays back and I straddle his hips, taking charge of the situation. I slide my hands across his chest, and consider leaning down to lick the lines of his abs. The vee of his hips taunt my drunken mind.

Instead, I start at his ear, leaving a line of kisses down his neck stopping the hollow of his throat. Here, I alternate licks and kisses as I move across his shoulder. He groans then wraps me in his arms as he rolls us over. His smile is encouraging as he says, "My turn."

He kisses me so sweetly, my heart starts to ache. My brain decides now is a good time to chastise me for falling into bed with him because I'm drunk. The free spirit that resides inside is quick to shut that bitch up. We want this. He's hot, and it has been five years.

Even back then, it wasn't special. It had been an obligation. A requirement. Something I'd had to do to keep my ex-husband happy so he wouldn't hurt me. Realizing I'm mentally checked out of this moment, I open my eyes to focus on Justin.

Moans slip out of me as he mimics the path of kisses I left on his body. The only difference is how his large, hot hands explore my body. He's careful as he slides his hands under my T-shirt, up from my waist, across my stomach, and my scar. The scar. *Oh No!* My mind starts screaming at me. *No no no! Stop!* Sobering, I grab his hand and yell, "Stop! Don't! No!"

Justin immediately stops and pulls back. He throws his hands in the air like a criminal that's been caught, "What's wrong? What did I do? Did I hurt you?" Concern colors across his face.

Pushing him off, I sit up, drawing my knees up to my chest. I rest my head on them as I try to catch my breath. He moves away from me, but only fractionally. He's quiet until my breathing normalizes.

"Hey," he says gently. "I'm sorry. It was too fast. We shouldn't have..."

I sigh. "Please, don't apologize. That was...I just..." I can't look at him. I can't finish the sentence. Tears pool and then start streaming down my face. I'm trying to regain some perspective and calm down. There's a shift as Justin stands up. I don't want him to leave, but I don't know how to tell him why I stopped him.

He starts moving around the room, dressing. He comes to the edge of the bed, runs his hand from the crown of my head, and down my back. He sits for a long while rubbing my back. I think he's waiting on me to snap out of it and talk to him. It seems like an eternity that he sits with me. Waiting.

Eventually, he kisses the top of my head, gets up from the bed, opens the door, and leaves.

When the door closes and his truck starts, the devastation of the moment becomes too much. I curl into a ball and fall apart.

4 - Trust

I wake from my usual nightmare, sweating in a freezing house, disoriented. The only thing that anchors me is the smell of fresh coffee wafting through the house. Instead of starting with my morning shower, I decide to talk to Kate. When I enter the kitchen, she turns and places a cup of coffee on the breakfast bar. I smile. She doesn't. She's busy making pancakes and eggs. Bacon is already done and sitting on some plates for us.

"Yum. Breakfast. Thanks, babe," I say to test the waters.

She lets out a small laugh. "Oh, you know this doesn't come cheap. We are going to talk about last night."

Her answer tells me all I need to know about the way this conversation is going to go. I consider the whole story of my past. Guilt courses through me as it occurs to me that I shouldn't have gone to the bar last night. I should have just gone to see Irma. Justin wouldn't have been in my bed, and I wouldn't be shattered because he left. I wouldn't be frustrated by my reaction to him touching my scar. The first guy I've gotten near, and I ruined it.

I'm startled out of my thoughts when Kate puts a plate in front of me. I look up into her eyes. Her face softens as she reaches out to wipe tears from my cheeks. "Hey, are you okay? Did he hurt you?"

I smile. "No. He's so perfect, it's ridiculous. I'm okay, I think. Did you sleep with Cam?"

The look on her face is an answer without actually answering.

"Jesus, woman! You aren't wasting time are you? How was it?" I wink.

Her Cheshire grin expands. "I mean, I'm no connoisseur of penises, but I've seen a few in my time."

"Define 'a few.'"

She chuckles. "Um, three-to-fifteen."

I gape. "And?"

"And Cameron is pretty great. We'll talk about you and Justin tonight." The look she gives me is one my mother would have given me. I know better than to argue with her. "Eat up. It'll get cold."

I do as I'm told and don't attempt to talk to her right now. There's too much at stake. Maybe I can see Irma and get some direction on how to handle this.

৪০৫৪৪০৫৪৪০৫৪৪০৫৪৪০৫৪৪০৫৪

Work is going well today. Surprisingly so. When things go this well, I wait for the other shoe to drop. *Something is going to happen.* My mind always nags at me when things are too good.

It's been a habit my whole life. Focusing on what's happening at work is exactly what I need to distract me from the prior night's events.

What was I thinking? I know what I was thinking. I was thinking *God, he's hot, his hands are so warm,* and *he certainly is skilled at using that tongue.* Thanks, beer, for making me forget I've sworn off involvement with men. What happened last night is why. Lost in thought, I don't notice my prospective new manager, Dee, standing by my cube. She clears her throat and I jump.

"Alana! I'm sorry, hun. I didn't mean to spook you."

Holding my heart inside my chest with both hands, I take a deep breath, and try to reassure her. "No, it's my fault. I was thinking about something else."

She smiles. "Deep thoughts, huh?"

"Something like that. What can I do for you?"

"Well, I just wanted to tell you that we are going to wait to make a decision on that job. It's going to be another week. We have a strong external candidate we'd like to meet with."

"Okay," my voice is small.

Now, it's her turn to try and reassure me, "I know it's not what you wanted to hear, but I wanted to keep you apprised."

"I appreciate it. Thank you."

Dee leaves and I notice that it's about lunch time. Life has been so insane the last couple of days, I think I need to follow up on my visit to Irma. Something has been nagging me to go see her. Even though it's a little early, I grab my purse, and head out.

When I pull up in her driveway, Irma steps out on to the porch. *She knew I was coming,* I think. I never thought I would believe in the things she says, or says she can do. Seeing first-hand changed my opinion on the matter. I bolt up the porch steps as fast as possible. I'm careful not to knock her over as I barrel toward her and hug her sweet neck. She squeezes me back as hard as she can.

"Girl, get in this house. It's cold ya know!"

"Yes, ma'am." Irma is not to be argued with. Ever.

Irma closes the door behind us and starts immediately, "What's going on? Get to talkin'. You ain't got much time."

"How do you know?"

"Trust me. You ain't my first adopted child. I've adopted so many wayward children over the years, I can spot a problem following you before you know it's there. Lord knows when you need me, and that's what I'm here for, so start talkin'!"

I don't hold back. There's no reason to; she knows the worst things about me. I start spilling about everything that happened last night. Justin, the bar, the bed, and how it all ended. She's made me a sandwich for lunch while I was talking. She places it on the table in front of me and orders me to eat.

While I do as I'm told, she gives me her two cents, "Listen here. Ya know better than ta go drinking and bring a man home. Especially one you've only known a day, but I ain't here ta preach. You take care of that business."

I nod appropriately as she continues, "What ya need right now is ta trust someone. You have ta let go of the shame your ex put in your head. What happened ta you wasn't your doin'. Start with that roommate of yours. She's good people. Let her in; it'll start your heart ta healin'. If he's worth it, you'll find yourself wanting to tell him all about your past. Ya have ta give the man a chance. He's not your ex."

"Irma, I swear it doesn't feel like I've known him only a day. It feels like I've known him forever. There's something about him that nags the back of my mind. That 'I know you from somewhere' feeling."

"In my experience, that means you knew him in another life. But, baby, you've had a couple lives in just this life. Ya going ta let what's-her-name in on your secret? It's a good way ta test trusting someone."

"What's the point? Does it really change anything?"

"Child, I tell you what I can when I can. Right now, if I told you everything, you'd go and mess it all up. I ain't lettin' that happen."

In the end, I agree to try trusting someone. Irma studies my palm before letting me leave. She mumbles under her breath, but as usual, she refuses to explain what she's said. I've learned to quit worrying about that. She's just Irma, and I trust her. "Irma, tell me how you're feeling."

"Don't you go worryin' 'bout me, ya hear?"

"Oh, I don't worry. Cade does. He asks me to keep up with you. I don't do a very good job of it, normally. Which means that unless I call Rhae and Cade soon, they'll make a trip up here to check on you."

I've ruffled her feathers because she starts on a rant about minding your own business, which is followed by a fit about Cade and Rhae working on babies instead of fussing over her. Finally, she settles on telling me to tell them she's fine.

I nearly agree, but remind her that they won't buy a "fine" update. They know she's been feeling down a bit lately. Mostly, we all think it's seasonal. She can't get out and about too much during winter and ever since her husband passed, she's even less inclined to do anything outside of her house.

She relents and tells me about her most recent doctor's appointments. Which she swears are all good. I promise to fill in Cade and Rhae when I talk to them. She fusses some more and forces me to take her extra pair of gloves before leaving.

On the way back to the office, I call Kate on my cell. She's cleared her calendar for tonight so we can spend some quality time together.

"I was planning to corner you until you talked anyway. So I told the ladies I have some personal business to handle."

The ladies are her roller derby team. The actual team name is the Derbytaints. The mascot is a busty girl holding a beer, pinky out, of course. They scare me to death because, on the one hand, I wish I was bold enough to play a sport so intense. On the other hand, the skill it takes to play that sport isn't just physical. It's a mental game, too. Suffice to say, I have immense respect for the ladies.

"Thank you for backing out of team dinner for me. You won't get benched during the bout for missing it will you?"

"Nah. Cap said for me to bring my personal business to the bout and she'll forgive me."

"Um, Kate, what do they think your personal business is?"

"Duh, a man."

I can't help the raucous laughter that bubbles up. It's very Kate to blow something off to get laid.

"Well, I'm not putting out. Just dinner, ya hear?" I mimic Irma's favorite expression and tone of voice.

"You'll put out. It's Taco Tuesday!"

"Damn! I just might. Hey, listen, I need to talk to Justin too. Do you mind if we eat early so I can make time for him?"

Her huff on the other end of the line lets me know she's not down with sharing me tonight. "Why does he get to intrude on our night?"

I sigh. "You'll understand after we talk. Love ya. Don't forget to pick up beans."

I walk into the office feeling lighter from the idea of letting just a tiny bit of this burden go. As I turn the corner toward my cube, I see Justin working on a copier.

He's squatting close to the floor, elbows-deep in the machine's guts. He looks up as I'm appreciating the level of effort he's putting into the job at hand.

His smile is kind. It strikes me as a little sympathetic, but I try to shake it off. It's a negative feeling that will do nothing to help me remedy the situation. I dig deep for a broad, genuine smile, and I walk over to him.

He stands to greet me, and I notice he has toner or some other nasty mechanic-looking junk on his hands. When he starts to speak, I hold up my hand to silence him. "We'll talk tonight."

He nods and says, "Is this a conversation I want to have, or should we just go our separate ways now?"

I step closer to him and wrap my arms around his waist, close my eyes, lay my head on his chest. His heartbeat pounds under my ear, and I hold him until he reciprocates the embrace, which he does with his forearms so he doesn't get toner all over me. I take a deep breath. "You want to have it."

He drops his head to rest on top of mine. "Okay."

Looking up into his eyes, I explain, "I have dinner with Kate tonight. Shouldn't take too long. Dare I suggest we meet somewhere to talk after?"

He smiles. "Sure. As long as it's not the bar, I think I'm good with wherever."

"You know, I don't usually take guys home from the bar, right?"

He chuckles. "No, I didn't know that. I hardly know you at all. It's been what?" He checks his watch. "Thirty-six hours since you finally told me your name?" It's a question and a statement.

I purse my lips and attempt to pout, but that doesn't last more than a split-second. "What if I told you I feel like I've known you for far longer than thirty-six hours? I can't remember how or where we met, but there's something there; right below the surface. Cheesy, huh?"

His expression is of pure relief. "God! I'm so glad you said it first!"

The corner of my mouth turns up in a smile. "Totally cheesy. My friend says it means we knew each other in another life. I don't know if I believe in that kind of stuff, but it's an interesting thought."

The smile on his face broadens. "I like that. Past lives, *ooooooh*. So, talking tonight after dinner?"

"Yes. Absolutely. How do I get in touch with you?"

He laughs and reminds me he has a cell phone. Pulling a cloth from his back pocket, he cleans his hands and then hands me his cell phone from his front pocket.

I create a new contact with my information for him. When I hand the phone back, I look around us to see if we have audience. We don't. I stand on tip-toes and plant a quick kiss on his delectable mouth. His smile as I walk away is all I need to get me through the rest of the day.

ଔ୯୫ଔ୯ଔ୯ଔ୯ଔ୯ଔ୯ଔ

Dinner with Kate is amazing. When I walked through the door this evening, she already had the tacos well in-hand. We haven't had Taco Tuesday in a month or so, and the smell is mouth-watering.

"We really need Taco Tuesday on a weekly basis. This is too good not to do it once a week," I observe.

"Agreed. Do you want a Corona?" Kate asks. She decided that Coronas were the only beer we should be drinking with the gloriousness that is Taco Tuesday.

"Absolutely. Update me on the asshole at work."

"Well," she drags the word out as she pops the caps off our beers and comes back to the table. "Today, I had a talk with HR about him. Son of a bitch laid his hands on me."

I nearly choke on my tortilla chip. "What? He had the balls to put his hands on you at work?"

She nods. "Yeah. You know how we have that little room beside the cubes that has our copier and office supplies in it? Well, I went in there to make some copies. While the machine was running, I was digging through the small accessory supplies looking for tiny binder clips. I was leaning over the drawer, and I heard the door close. At first, I thought a draft or something that had pushed it closed. When I turned around, there he was. He is such a slime ball. He tries to come off all preppy, uber-professional, and ends up looking like an overpaid pimp."

I reach across the table to grab her hand.

Kate takes a deep breath, and continues, "Anyway, I asked him if he needed anything. The look he gave me made all the hairs on my neck stand up. I started running through my mind what I would do if he touched me."

Tears fill her eyes, and she takes a moment to gather herself. "When he moved in closer, I froze. Shit, Alana, I just locked the fuck up! I had it in mind that I would use the three-hole punch on the shelf to knock him out or something. When the time to act was upon me, I fucking froze."

When she finishes, she tanks half her beer in one swallow.

"Hey, it's okay. None of us knows how we'll react in that situation. It's not supposed to happen." I try to sound reassuring.

"Yeah. I know," she wipes a tear from her cheek, takes a breath, and finishes the story. "So anyway, he leaned into me, and I could smell that cheap-ass aerosol cologne he wears. I was about to gag because it was so strong. I pulled back and managed to ask him to let me by. As I went to move by him, he snaked his arm around my waist and grabbed my ass. He whispered in my ear, 'I love dark meat. Go ahead tell HR this happened. It'll be your word against mine.' I pulled away from him and ripped the door open. I was so freaked that I forgot to get my copies off the machine. I went straight to the bathroom to calm down. When I got back to my desk, my copies were in my chair with a sticky note that said, 'I own you.'"

"Kate! That is some scary shit. Tell me you took the note to HR immediately!" My blood is boiling for her.

"I did. I went to see a lady named Caroline. She said there's no security cameras in the copy room. Then she said the note could have been from anyone. She offered to have a strong conversation with him. I couldn't help but laugh at her. Does she really think that will do anything but piss him off? When he gets pissed off, what happens to me then?"

My agreement is swift, "Well, what's she going to do about it?"

Kate looks defeated, "She can't do anything. No one saw anything. The story can't be corroborated beyond my statement. He was right. It is he said/she said."

"I'm sorry. Anything I can do?"

She grins. "Yeah. Get promoted so I can take your old job!"

"Working on it, sister."

"Enough about my bullshit. Talk," she orders.

I start with a deep breath. "How much detail do you want?"

Her look is pointed. "Do you even need to ask that question? I want all of it."

Pushing back from my food, I grab my beer for liquid support. "Okay, well, I met Justin at work on Monday. Yesterday. He works for the company that manages all of our IT and hardware stuff—printers and whatnot. I was trying to fix the printer that eats all of my stuff when I ripped a lever off of it. He laughed at me, and I was pissed. Later, he found me and apologized."

I take a drink from my beer before going on, "So things get a little odd when I see him at the deli where the girls and I had lunch. One of those moments, like, 'Okay, saw you earlier. Hey there, handsome.' And then moving on. Then we were at the bar, and you saw how that went. Fast forward to when we left the bar. He brought me home, and I threw myself at him. Something about that unruly hat hair and the smell of his leather jacket..."

"And that he's fucking hot, and you were drunk as shit...go on."

"Hey, bitch, my story. Yes, he's hot, and I was drunk. Maybe a little horny. It's been five years, Kate. Did I ever tell you that?"

The look that passes over her is nothing short of shock and awe. "How the hell have you gone five years without getting laid? I mean, not even a one-nighter? There's nothing wrong with you. You're gorgeous, albeit a little standoffish with men. I can see where it would take a special guy to break through your resting bitch face, but five years? Seriously?"

I try for a look that says, *I will cut you*. I think she gets it because she uses her fingers in a zipper motion to indicate that she'll shut up until I finish.

Raising my eyebrows, I start again, "Can I finish now? Anyway, as I was saying, I basically jumped him. He was all-too-willing. We ended up in my bed, he was half- stripped. I was out of my jeans, but not my top. When he went to remove my shirt, I freaked out. I pushed him away and started crying."

"Why?" she asks, concern etched on her face as her brows pull in to form a crease between her eyes.

I sigh. "There's a lot you don't know about me." I shake my head. "This part I need to show you." I stand from the chair and lift the hem of my work blouse to show her my scar. Kate gasps, and comes around to my side of the table for a closer look. She runs her hand over the bubbled up tissue.

"What the fuck is that?"

"Sit down. There's a whole other story to tell you. I've only shared this with one other person: Ms. Irma. There's a lot to absorb. You will want to sit for this."

I start telling her about my life with Kent. I tell her about Ethan, and I can't help crying when I do. She holds my hand and gives gentle squeezes to keep me talking. It's comforting.

She wants to know, and I need her to, so I keep talking. It takes a few minutes, but I finally get around to telling her about that night. The night when I died. Kate cries. I cry. She holds me, and I hold her.

"So when he touched your scar, something came back to you?" she asks.

I nod. "Yeah. You could say that. I haven't been with a man since it happened. Letting him touch me, let alone see it, it was all too much. I freaked."

"You need to tell him."

"Maybe."

Something occurs to her, and she asks, "So the nightmares?"

"Yeah. They start when I wake up covered in blood. They are always the same. I run from the trailer, through the woods, and out on to the road. They always end with me in a truck begging a stranger for help. I never see his face though. It's more like I feel him. I feel safe in the truck. So I think that's when my mind relaxes and I wake up."

Kate thinks for a minute. "Have you ever considered counseling?"

I shake my head. "Definitely not. You are only the second person in my life to know any of this."

"Thank you for trusting me, but with the freak out and the nightmares, maybe it's time to talk to someone."

"I am. You. I actually feel much better now that you know."

"One of the girls on my team is a counselor who works with battered women. If you decide you need someone to talk to, I can give you her number. I'll stay out of it, and she can be totally confidential about it."

"I really appreciate it. I'm not ready yet, but maybe one day."

We talk for a while longer, and finish off a few more beers. Then Kate and I wash the dishes. I change into jeans and a T-shirt to go meet up with Justin. As I'm getting ready, I get a text. *"Everything okay? Are we still talking tonight?"*

I can't help grinning while I text him back. *"A little excited, are we? :) Yeah. Still on. Where?"*

His answer is nearly instant. *"My place. 330 Vine. When?"*

It takes me a few minutes to answer. Do I really want to do this at his place? What could happen? I mean he'll probably kick me out after I tell him how damaged I am. Nobody wants to deal with this type of baggage. I answer him, *"Thirty minutes."*

As I finish dressing, I think through the story and what I should or should not tell him. By the time I'm walking out the front door, I've decided the only way this thing can work is to tell him all of it.

5 - Shame

The hardest part of telling Justin is going to be the shame. Unless someone has been through what I've been through, they don't understand the shame and guilt of surviving. The drive to his house is faster than I thought it would be. I had to use the map function on my phone to find it. Turns out his house is in a neighborhood a few miles from ours. I pull in the driveway, and, just like Irma, he steps out onto the porch to greet me. Justin doesn't stop on the porch, though; he comes to the car, and opens the door for me.

I start to think he's just chivalrous, but then he nearly pulls me from the car. His embrace is warm and snug. "Come inside, it's freezing," he says into the top of my head.

Shaking my head, I mumble into his chest, "It's not freezing where I am."

He laughs, releases me, and leads me up the steps to his house. I walk in like a kid exploring. I can't help but look around like I've entered some museum display. It's a tribute to post-frat, disorganized, modern American male living.

Truly a study in how to survive with a sink full of dishes right up to the cabinet line and clothing piled in lines down the hallways like snow drifts. There are small foot paths that shows someone actually moves around the piles of gross.

Justin doesn't stop in the common living area he takes me down the laundry-lined hallway all the way to the end.

There are two doors facing each other at the dead end, and double doors at the head of the hallway. I assume, based on most floor plans, this is the unused laundry closet. Justin opens the door on the left, and says proudly, "My room."

Still in analytical mode, I'm prepared to scrutinize yet more piles of dishes and dirty everything, but I'm more than surprised to see that his room is not only tidy, but immaculate. No dust, shoes are organized in a cubby shelf, hats hang on a rack behind the closet door, and a sweet desk where he has dual monitors setup next to a docked laptop.

"Impressive," I observe.

He shrugs. "Doesn't take much to impress when you have to walk through Cameron's hell to get here."

I laugh. "True story. So I take it that"—I indicate the living room by throwing my thumb over my shoulder to point at the door—"is all Cameron."

He raises his eyebrows and purses his lips into a flat line. "You got it. Kid's a mess."

"Uh, kid? You guys are the same age."

He grins. "Physically, not mentally. Certainly not in terms of maturity. Hang on, let me fetch you a chair. Cam doesn't use his desk chair."

I start to argue that we could sit on the bed, but then I reconsider because if we sit on that bed, this conversation is over before it can begin. I'm really pissed at myself for not having better self-control around him. It is ridiculous when I think about it. I'm rolling my eyes as I pace his room, and he catches me.

"Rolling your eyes already? We haven't even started."

I laugh. "Oh just having a mental conversation with myself. You know self-control and whatnot."

He nods. "I had the same conversation with myself before you pulled up." Sliding his desk chair out to me, he takes the one brought in from Cam's room. I'm grateful because Cam's chair looks like its seen better days.

I slide my jacket off and lay it on his bed alongside my purse. He waits for me to sit, and then takes his own seat. I can't make eye contact with him. It's too awkward. I fidget.

Finally, he reaches out and covers my hands with his own. "Talk to me."

I take a breath, look at him, and feel a crater open in my chest. I fight the panic and simply say, "I'm trying to figure out where to start."

"Start at the beginning," he says by way of solution.

Stinging builds in my eyes, and I know I'm going to cry, despite my efforts to stave it off. "If only it were that easy. There's a lot."

Justin looks puzzled, and seems to be thinking of something. He squeezes my hands. "Okay. So let's start with last night. What happened?"

I shrug. "I, uh, I...panicked. The easiest way to explain it is that I haven't been with someone for a very long time. I think being drunk, the chemistry we have, the opportunity...I don't know. It all added up to bad decisions."

His eyebrows raise. "I'm a bad decision?"

"Oh, God, no! I just mean that maybe it wasn't a good idea to fall into bed with you on the first day I met you. Especially when I'm drinking. Drinking and taking any guy home is a bad decision. Not you. I think you are the good decision. You were good enough to recognize something wasn't right. You didn't take advantage of me or the situation. What I need to tell you about my past is ..." I trail off, trying to find the right words. "I'm not sure how you'll take it."

He looks away from me, defeated. "So, you're not even giving me a chance."

Shock hits me. This is going all wrong. "I *am* giving you a chance. That's why I'm here. I think you are worth more than a one-nighter, as Kate calls them. Am I wrong?"

He shakes his head. "Nope. I'm gold, baby. I'm worth being an every-nighter."

"You certainly don't lack confidence," I say sarcastically. We both laugh. "But I think you're right. That's why I'm here."

His eyes soften as his smile fades. "What I don't understand is why you freaked? I want to understand what happened to send you into all-out physical panic. Baby, you seriously shut down."

"I need a drink. Do you have anything stronger than beer?"

His mouth twists in a thoughtful expression. "I have vodka in the freezer. Will that work?"

I shake my head. "Getting drunk together didn't really work out last time."

"We won't get drunk. Cameron is working a late shift to pick up extra money. The house is ours. We have all night. We'll sip slowly and only when you need the courage."

Thinking it over, I nod. "Okay. Better run grab that vodka. We'll need it."

As soon as the words leave my mouth he moves like a jack-rabbit leaving the room. I hear cabinets closing, and feet pounding the hall. These old houses have crawlspaces instead of slab foundations, so every footstep resonates. You have to put extra effort into walking quietly. Justin is clearly not into expending the extra energy right now. When he returns, he has a box of cheese crackers, two shot glasses, and a bottle of top-shelf vodka.

"No cheap vodka for you, huh? You're big time."

"No, ma'am. If I'm drinking liquor, it's the best. Plus, the cheap shit burns going down. It tastes like kerosene." He sets everything on his desk and then kicks his boots off. "You don't mind if I get comfortable do you?"

Shaking my head, I answer, "Mind if I do the same?"

"Of course not. Make yourself at home."

Rolling my eyes, I remind him that I've only known him like a day and a half. Still, I reach down and untie my boots then slide them off. Taking my socks off, I turn them right side out and place them in my boots for safe-keeping. When I look up, Justin has moved to the bed. I look at him expectantly.

"What? Comfortable. Right?" he answers my unspoken question, then smiles his megawatt smile.

"Right." I answer.

He pats the bed beside him. "Come on up." He's nearly bouncing.

I hesitate, reminding myself that we've already had the self-control conversation. Then I decide the fact that we had the conversation means we're both committed to behaving ourselves and ignoring our baser instincts.

Oh, my God. I think as I walk over and sit on the edge of the bed. As soon as I do, he hands me a shot glass, which he fills with vodka. I take two shots back to back, and give the glass back to him. "Thanks." I slide up the bed to rest my back against his headboard. I snag one of his pillows and hug it.

I bury my face in it to get my thoughts together. My brain is like an ADHD squirrel right now. I'm waiting for the vodka to give me a little bit of relaxation. The pillow smells like him. It's not doing anything to help me settle down. Adrenaline is filling my veins as I war with myself. *I need to tell him. Trust him. But what if...*

The *what if* is what grips me. What if he wants nothing else to do with me? I'll be fine. How will it be different than before I met him?

I square my shoulders, and look at him. Then I just blurt it out, "I died."

Shock is the first look on his face, which resolves to determined patience. "What?"

I nod. "It's true. You are talking to someone who died and came back from the dead."

He looks dubious. "I'm going to need you to elaborate on that a bit more."

"I'm not really Alana Thomas. That's my name right now, but that's not who I am." He looks seriously confused. "Maybe I should start at the beginning now that you have the punchline."

I shift next to him on the bed and lean my shoulder against his. Looking him in the eye as I tell this story will do nothing but make this harder. I begin, "I got married when I was nineteen. He was older. I was raised in a really strict household. My parents were rigid conservatives. They had a million rules and routines for me to follow. The more they piled on, the more I rebelled. I bet you couldn't imagine I was a rebellious child." I smile, and he answers with a shake of his head.

"Not you." His sarcasm is on point tonight.

"Yeah, I know. Anyway, one night I'm out with my friends. We were hanging out on a bridge that ran over an irrigation ditch on some farm land. There were actually two bridges over that particular ditch. They were about a mile apart. There was the one we were on to drink, and the other was used for, well...you get it. Anyway, we would watch for headlights and hide our beers when we saw a car coming. You see, we were in a dry county, so if the cops caught us drinking, there were two options: the cop could confiscate the beer and run us off, or he could arrest every last one of us. What actually happened was based on the cop who caught us and whether or not he felt like doing paperwork and calling parents."

"So, we're out there drinking. We see headlights. Everyone hides their beers. The car parks behind one of ours, and a guy steps out. He announces that he's not a cop, and then says his name. Turns out one of my guy friends knew him. He graduated with my friend's older brother. You have to know, I grew up in a really small town in Mississippi. This was normal. Hell, it might still be normal. I haven't been back for a long while."

Justin is patiently listening. He's shifted so he's lying on his side, looking up at me, his elbow on the bed propping his head up with his hand. Every now and then as I talk, I turn to look at him to gauge his expression.

So far it's blank, like he's totally unsurprised by my unremarkable tale of small towns in Mississippi. On the one hand, I like it. On the other, I'm worried he's a great poker player; hiding his thoughts.

"We all resume our drinking. Some people are dancing and cozying up as the night is prolonged. I'm as drunk as I was last night when my friend introduces me to Kent Walsh."

Saying his name aloud gives me a chill. I swallow hard, ""We hit it off, I guess. He drove me home because my girlfriend wanted to go to the other bridge for some fun with her boyfriend. Within a week, we were an official item. He met my parents and charmed them. Something seemed off about him, but he was handsome, rich, and charismatic. He managed gain my parents to agreement to let me go on dates when previously they wouldn't let me out of their sight. I was seventeen years old when we met. What was I supposed to do?"

"Going out with him meant I didn't have to lie and sneak out anymore. They let me go with him, and at first, he was okay with hanging out with my friends, doing the things we were doing anyway. After a year, things started changing with him. He didn't want to hang out with my friends anymore. He didn't want to party. He wanted to take me to dinners with work colleagues. I felt special most nights. He insisted I dress in cocktail attire. My mother was impressed with his resources and his job, so she would go out of her way to make sure I was ready to go out with him. She spent more time, money, and attention on me while I was with Kent than she ever did before. All of a sudden, I was important."

"So even though I was feeling more distant from Kent most of the time, I sucked it up. My mom was happy. Dad seemed to like him," I finish, looking down at my hands. I know where this is going and it isn't happy.

Looking at Justin, he can tell things are ready to take a turn. "Drink?"

I nod. He obliges. Tossing back a shot, I hold the glass out for him to fill again. "Another."

"But we're not getting drunk, right?" he confirms.

"Right." I take another shot. Heat is creeping into my cheeks. The desired fuzzy brain and numb teeth affect is starting to build. I take a deep breath, and continue, "Early on, Kent and I had a great sex life. I wasn't a virgin when we got together, so it's not that kind of story. I didn't stay with him because he was my first or anything like that. I mean, from day one, we had great physical chemistry. It wasn't until later that our sex life became horrible, but I'll get to that."

"A couple of months after my nineteenth birthday, I skipped my period. Kent took me to the pharmacy and then to dinner. I took the pregnancy test in the bathroom of the restaurant to keep it from my parents. It was positive. I'm not sure how long I stayed in the bathroom, crying, but eventually Kent came in to get me."

"I had contemplated telling him it was negative and finding a way to get an abortion. Who the hell wants to be a wife and mother at the ripe, old age of nineteen? In the end, I couldn't hide it. I told him. He was excited. Elated even. He and I told my parents together. And you know what?"

Justin looks surprised. "What?"

"Those assholes, who had preached abstinence to me for years, were fucking ecstatic I'd gotten knocked up. I lost my mind. I actually stood up and screamed at all of them and then stormed off to my room. Kent stayed another hour talking to my parents."

"The next day, I was informed by my mother that we were going shopping for a wedding dress. That if we remedied it fast enough, no one at their prestigious church would know I'd gotten pregnant out of wedlock."

Justin interrupts, "Wait. What? They just up and decided what to do without asking you? They didn't get your opinion on being married? He didn't propose?"

"Nope. Getting pregnant made it not my decision in my family's eyes. Good southern girls who get pregnant out of wedlock, and have parents that have a reputation to uphold, get married. It was a bonus for them that Kent was rich and had an amazing job. The perfect man to make their daughter an honest woman. He was going to settle me down. They were thrilled at the idea that someone might be able to do that."

Incredulity being the winning expression of the day, Justin says, "So you married him. And you had a baby?"

I nod.

Still working it out, he asks, "How old are you now?"

I smile. "I recently turned twenty-eight."

"Was it a boy or a girl?" he asks.

"A boy. His name is Ethan. He would be eight now."

Puzzled he asks, "Would be?"

I nod. "Drink."

Serving me another shot of vodka, I take a deep breath and stand to pace. "You see, I am the worst mother ever. I left him when he was three. I left him with Kent."

"I'm sure you had your reasons."

Once again, he's right. I had plenty of reasons. Justin is seeing the tip of the iceberg. He wants to believe the best of me, and I think he's precious for it. I know the truth. I was a coward. My biggest regret in life is that I never stood up to Kent.

"I did. I died. You see, Kent was the worst husband I could have found. To my parents, and the rest of the world, he was an amazing, successful provider. At home, he changed. It all started to shift after we got married. I was four months pregnant when he took me to dinner. Morning sickness was more like all day sickness for me. I made the mistake of getting sick at the restaurant where we were having dinner with some of his colleagues. I spent a good bit of time in the bathroom, and turned down dessert offered by his boss."

I stop pacing when I think about the next part of this story. My breath hitches, and without looking at Justin, I continue, "When we got home, Kent beat me within an inch of my life. I was terrified. When he went to work the next day, I ran away to my parent's house.

"My mother assured me I had misunderstood him, and I likely did something to deserve getting beat. My rebellions were aggravating for him. She said I would need to settle down for the beatings to stop. She instructed me to make his favorite dinner to make it up to him. I did. That night Kent came home apologetic. He made promises about how it would never happen again. I believed him."

With a distant look in his eye, Justin says, "They always promise."

I don't understand what's happening with him. He's gone from warm and comforting to distant, almost cold, "Hey," I say.

He blinks a few times, and then looks at me.

"What's going on over there?" I ask.

He looks reluctant, and then says, "Nothing. Go on."

"By the time I was eight months pregnant, Kent wanted to take me away to Gulf Shores for a weekend. He set everything up, and surprised me when he came home from work. I was told to pack a small bag so we could leave immediately. The weekend seemed to go really well. He was kind, attentive, and passionate with me.

"On our last night there, he wanted to take me out for a 'fancy' dinner. I was trying to dress nice, but being the size of a house at the time, it was taking me too long. He got angry. As we were walking down the steps down from the B&B we were staying in, he pushed me. I don't remember anything between being on the stairs and waking up in the ER. When I came to, Kent was talking in hushed tones with the doctors who were assuring him the baby was fine. I started crying when I saw him."

I take a deep breath to steady myself. The hopelessness I'd felt for so long starts seeping back into my chest. "I told the nurse who was attending to me what happened. I told her I was afraid for my life and the life of my son. She seemed to believe me, but the doctor she reported to didn't believe it at all. Kent had him convinced that he was worried about a head injury. They performed numerous tests and ultimately released us for the drive back home. Kent could not have turned into a better actor after that. The birth of Ethan put him on cloud nine. He was so happy that I got nearly a year without being belittled or beaten. However, that's also about the time Kent started to lose his position at his company.

"There were layoffs, there was downsizing, and sales fell off. He was a salesman, and this was a bad deal for him. He spiraled. Kent was drunk every night of the week. He was violent and angry with me whenever he was drinking. I walked on eggshells all the time and made sure I had the house, baby, and dinner ready for his inspection and approval at all times."

The memory gives me pause. "It was a hell I could not have imagined for myself. Eventually, Kent lost his job, and we were forced to sell the house and move into a trailer on some land his family owned. He was in such a perpetual messy state of existence that I had no hope.

Justin is sitting stock still, cradling the bottle of vodka as I continue, "One night, when Ethan was three, Kent came home high as a kite. I had suspected he was using meth. This confirmed it. I confronted him about being fucked up. I didn't care about what he wanted anymore. I demanded a divorce. I told him I was done with his bullshit.

His response was to beat shit out of me. At one point during the fight, he hit me so hard I flew across the room into the bookcase. It knocked me unconscious. When I woke up, he was passed out on the couch surrounded by empty beer cans. Ethan had spent the night with my parents, so I knew he was safe.

"At first, I couldn't move. I thought it was because of how hard he had hit me. I was taking a mental inventory of my body to see if anything was broken when I ran my hand across my stomach. I had been shot. I was bleeding a ton. The memory of the gun being fired came back to me. Initially, terror filled me, and then I thought to myself that I have two choices: I can lay here and die—give up and let go—or I can find some way to get on my feet and leave.

"That's the only way I would survive is to leave. It took every ounce of courage and strength I had, but I did it. I got up and I ran. I ran across a field and through some woods until I came to an old country road. Usually, there is no one driving that road in the middle of the night. But I prayed. I prayed for God to send someone to help me."

Justin clears his throat. "And he did," he says quietly.

I nod. "He did. I don't know who he was, but I climbed into his truck. The last thing I remember before waking up in the hospital is praying the guy driving that truck wouldn't kill me. Not like there was anything I could do about it. I think it was the blood loss or the exertion, but I passed out mid-prayer." Numbly, I wipe the tears from my cheeks I didn't realize I was crying. "And that's the night I died."

I finish and sit quietly to let Justin process what I've told him. He's eerily quiet and still. I watch him. He's not looking at me or doing anything really. While it feels good to have it in the open, his reaction is what I feared all along. He's freaking out.

"Say something. Please."

He doesn't. It's my turn to sit patiently and wait for the panic to pass. I'm waiting for a reaction or more questions. Neither comes. Deciding I've embarrassed myself enough for one night, I slip my socks and boots on and pick up my jacket. It's my turn to leave.

6 - Time

Two days pass. I haven't had any nightmares, and I haven't heard from Justin either. I don't know what I expected, but I had hoped at some point he would have called or texted me. I guess it was too much for him.

Kate bursts into my room. "Wake up! You're going to be late."

I laugh. "I'm not going to be late. This is my usual alarm time."

"What? You never have to wake up with an alarm." Her expression shifts from panicked friend to saucy friend.

I shrug and force a timid smile.

"Whatever!" She exclaims as she storms to the door. Turning back to me, she says, "We'll talk over breakfast. Hurry up!"

I shower and dress for work. Applying a little bit of makeup, I think how Irma was right, as always. At some point, I need to call her. The thought reminds me that I owe Rhae a call to update her on Irma's health.

Kate makes breakfast. I tell her how I left Justin stunned after our chat, and that I haven't heard from him since. She is lost for words, which is just weird for Kate. I dismiss myself before it can get any weirder and head to work.

Work is typical. The only exception is how light I feel as I breeze around doing all my normal daily tasks. Although, I haven't seen Justin, I'm all the better for having told him.

For the first couple of days, I feared I would see him, or that he would tell someone else and the rumor-mill would get cranked up. It hasn't happened, and I know I'm over-thinking it.

When lunch rolls around, I consider a mad dash to Irma's house again, but think better of it. Instead, I decide to eat alone and give Rhae a call. As I approach the café a few blocks from work, I hear a voice that sparks a memory. Fear lances through my heart, and I stop walking. *"It can't be!"* I turn toward the sound of the voice, and that's when I see Kent.

I plaster myself flat against the wall of the building and peer around as he's leaving the office building next to the café. His hair is longer, and slicked back. Other than that, it doesn't seem that the last five years have affected him. He's shaking hands with a man in a suit. They exchange pleasantries, and Kent walks down the street in the opposite direction from me. My knees falter, and I feel myself sliding toward the ground. My brain spirals into old memories, and I know that it was really him. I didn't imagine him. Holding my stomach, I can feel the scar through the material of my blouse. Nausea builds as I sit. I mentally chant my mantras.

I lay my head on my knees and pull my hair up off my neck. I need some air. *Breathe, breathe, breathe.* I keep swallowing to stop the nausea that's building. Telling Justin about him must have raised the damn devil himself. I think I might pass out when I'm brought back to the present by a woman asking me if I'm okay. *Am I okay?* I shake my head.

"No." My answer is barely audible. It's as if the air has been forced from my lungs and I don't have the strength to pull in more.

"Should I call someone? Do you need an ambulance?" the woman asks.

"No. Please. I'm okay." My words come a little stronger than before. The woman offers me her hand, and she helps me to my feet. I explain that I haven't eaten today, and I'm just a little light-headed. She accepts this excuse, and allows me to leave. I walk back to work, forgetting about lunch. In the office, I go to the Dragon Lady, tell her I'm sick and I'm going home. I don't wait for her answer or permission; I don't need it.

When I get home, I'm paranoid about locking up the house. I lock the front door, my bedroom door, and finally, I stumble into the bathroom, locking that door too. Alone in my bathroom, I climb into the empty bathtub and bury my face in my hands. Sobs rack my body. *How can he still affect me this much after all this time? Is it him or the memory of what he did?* I know the answer, but my mind is jumbled as I work through the fear that paralyzes me.

He didn't see me. He wouldn't recognize me if he did. My hair is a natural-looking red. It matches my skin tone well enough. I grew up with brown hair. Kent and my parents always had rules about coloring it, so they would have no idea what I look like now.

Plus, I've lost some weight and put on muscle. I'm sure Kent, if he was looking right at me, would still be looking for that mousey, chunky woman with limp brown hair. I was a shell of myself when I left. He had me on crazy diets because I still had some chunk from the baby.

Still, it was no excuse, and Kent Walsh would not have a fat wife. That would just not do. Shaping up in the last five years was my way of developing my self-esteem. Finding my own personal identity.

It made me feel good to work out. It made me feel alive when my legs and arms would shake with full exertion. The tears are drying, and I'm finding it easier to breathe as I relive the moments that made me better.

I hear Kate come into the house she's calling my name. Unsure of what time it is, I can only tell I've been here for far too long because my legs have gone numb, and my face feels scorched and dry because of the tears. Kate knocks on my bedroom door. "You in there?"

"Yeah. Give me a minute," I call out in response.

She stops knocking, and I turn on the shower. I need to straighten myself up before I face her. If she sees me like this, there's no telling what she might say or do. I don't want to explain that I'm a panicky, paranoid, freak to her.

I've been hiding my potential for panic so well. During my shower, I start making plans to move. I started over once, I can do it again. Kate would understand. Maybe. Justin definitely won't.

Does he matter enough to be considered in this decision? The thought feels like a hole in my chest. I obviously want him to matter, but he's checked out on me already.

We're talking life and death here, I reason with myself. Kent will fucking kill me if he finds me. Memphis is a big city, but apparently not big enough. What's he doing here anyway? Who was that man? What do they do in that building? The water runs cool, and I decide to get out and dress.

I slip into my flannel PJ bottoms and T-shirt as I go into my bedroom. My phone is on the bed vibrating. I check it and see that Justin has been texting and calling. Someone at work told him I went home sick. *So he was at our building today.* Although comforting, it's not enough to make me smile. I don't answer him, instead I head into the kitchen to grab some food with Kate. There are appearances to maintain, after all. And I may have given her the impression I'm one hundred percent well-adjusted after recovering from Kent. Slipping my "everything is okay" mask in place, I make a glass of wine and sit down at the table.

Kate picked up Chinese food on her way home, and she's scooping rice onto a couple of plates. She knows I love sweet and sour chicken with just plain rice. Fried rice ends up with onions no matter how many times I say "no onion." Fact of life. When she sets my plate in front of me, I manage a small, "thank you." She only nods.

Halfway through dinner, it's killing her. "What's up with you today?"

I shrug. "I don't know. Just a long day. Feeling kind of blah."

She gives me a knowing smile. "Been there. Asshole pulled his shit again today."

I drop my fork. "What? Did he touch you again?"

Small tears form in the corners of her eyes. "You could say that." Her answer is barely a mutter.

"Kate! Someone has to stop him. You have to report him again." My demand is emphatic.

Her voice is still small, "I did. The director of HR is investigating him."

Anger for what is happening to my friend replaces the fear I've been masking. "What happened?"

She goes on to tell me how he cornered her in the copy room again. This time he locked the door, and prevented her from leaving. He groped her and threatened to kill her if she told anyone again. He'll convince anyone that investigates him that she was the aggressor. Kate is tough, but she's not above being terrified by that kind of threat. Especially since his plan of evading investigation includes her own thoughts on the matter. Like the son-of-a-bitch can read her mind and validated her fears. He's also used his position to intimidate her; good ole boy manager vs female admin.

"He has to have done this before. I mean he's escalating. It can't be his first time trying this."

She shrugs. "I don't know. He's been at the company less time than I have. I don't know where he worked before."

I nod. I wish I knew a lawyer who could help her. This is sexual harassment to the extreme. He has put his hands on her and has now gone beyond the pale by threatening to kill her.

"You're not going to work tomorrow. Neither am I."

She grins around her tears and agrees. "Ice cream and Netflix?" she asks.

"Yes." I need a day to get my head together. She needs a day to let HR solve her problems.

While we discuss taking a girls' day to ourselves, Justin texts again. *"Please, just tell me you're okay?"*

Involuntarily, a small smile slips I shake my head at the phone like he can see it. *Oh, I wish I could tell you how not okay I am right now.* But I don't dare text him that. I get the feeling he would go all protective if I went into the entire story about how freaked I am about Kent. Kate needs me and I haven't made up my mind what Justin and I are at this point.

I text him back. *"I'm good. Thanks for checking on me."*

His answer is fast, *"Of course! I was hoping to see you tonight. Is it too late?"*

We need to cool it down for a while. I reply, *"Yeah, too late tonight. Maybe we can do something this weekend?"*

The little bubbles that dance on the screen let me know that he's typing a response. They flash on and off. On and off. Geez, he's struggling with what to say. This is all my fault. I shouldn't have led him on like I did. Finally, his response arrives, *"Yeah. Text me."*

It's a cold, non-committal response. While it's good he's texting, finally, it's probably going to end in a friendship. He still hasn't said anything about my confessions.

ഇരു☾ഇ☾ഇരു☾ഇ☾ഇരു☾ഇ☾ഇരു

Kate and I wake up at our usual times. I don't need the alarm to get up because the nightmares are back. Only they're worse than they've been in a very long time. During the replay last night, I think I could smell the smoke from the gunshot and hear the booming sound of it again. I'm able to shake off the sweats and settle myself down before Kate gets up.

We decided to call in at the same time. We used the same story about Chinese takeout (true), and getting some kind of food poisoning that showed up in the wee hours of the morning (lie). I think of it as a necessary evil so she and I can pull our shit together. She can't face the guy harassing her, and I can't face Justin.

I picture his face in my mind when I think of his name. The face I see is the one lying underneath me as I was exploring his body during our near-miss sexportunity. He was all smiles with a touch of curiosity. He trusted me, but I never gave it back. No, I panicked on him. The thought makes me a little sad. That was likely the one and only opportunity we would have.

After we finish calling in, we both go back to bed. Sleeping late is priority one on a girls' sick day. I'm not sure how it goes for Kate, but I can't sleep. I toss and turn, wrap myself in the blanket, throw the blanket off, and even go to the bathroom because my brain has convinced me that this is the problem. It was not the problem.

Sitting in the bed, I have my phone in my lap. It's silent. Nothing on text, nothing on social media. Nothing. I've been back in the bed for over two hours, and I can't stop thinking about Justin. He's my problem. I decide to clear my head by calling Rhae. I've been putting that off for a few days now.

She answers on the third ring, "Miles Construction."

"What, no hello?" I say jokingly.

Her whole tone changes. "Hey girl! How've you been?"

I laugh. "That's better. That's my Rhae-Rhae. I'm good. How's Cade?"

"Hot, as usual. What's the latest in big ole M-town?"

I sigh. "Not much. Too much."

"That," she starts and then pauses, "doesn't sound good. What's going on? Dragon Lady being a crazy bitch again?"

"Oh, how I wish this was as simple as the crazy bitch. No, there's a guy involved." I imagine the shock that crosses her face when I mention a guy. She knows I haven't dated in forever, but she doesn't know why.

"Dude, I thought you were gay."

I laugh way too hard. "Um, no. You know better. How many sex conversations have we had? Shady Ladies, remember?"

She slips into logical Rhae mode. "Just because you have a lot of experience with men doesn't mean that you aren't into women right now."

Laughing. "I'll keep that in mind. It is certainly an alternative to being with asshole guys."

"So tell me about this guy," she demands.

There's a long stretch of silence as I consider what I should say. What can I say? I've known him for less than a week. Hell. "His name is Justin Ellis. He works for the new hardware services tech company. I met him on Monday."

It's her turn to be silent as she processes. "Wait, this past Monday? Literally four days ago, and he's a problem already?"

I'm quiet when I respond, "Yeah. I know."

"He must be amazingly hot to tie you up in knots like this. Wait! Does he want to tie you up? Is that the problem?"

"Rhae! Where do you come up with this shit? No. He hasn't offered to tie me up."

Her laughter is comforting. "I was kidding. You sounded like you were getting all contemplative and sad over there. Just shaking you up. So what's the problem?"

I proceed to tell her about our drunken encounter, how I made a trip to see Irma, and Irma's advice about trying to trust someone.

Which only brought us around to the elephant in the room. "What made you so weary of trusting men?" Rhae asks. Perceptive as always. Practice makes perfect. So for the third time this week, I'm telling someone my long-held secret, and then I fill her in on what happened yesterday when I saw Kent on the street.

"Did you tell anyone you saw Kent?"

"No. I have everyone convinced I'm okay."

"First thing you need to do is make someone aware that he's close. What if he saw you? Things could get ugly fast. Promise me you will tell someone. Don't be a statistic because you're dumb. Secondly, you did the right thing by talking to Irma. She knows things about how to put broken lives back together. Trust me on this one, sweetie. So what now? Are you going to tell him?"

"I already did," my answer is quick. "I haven't seen him since. I think he's weirded out. As I expected."

"What was it you once said to me? Let him decide for himself if he wants to be with you? Maybe he's weirded out in the 'I need to deal' way. Not the 'I'm running far away from crazy' way."

I close my eyes. "I may have said that once. Clearly, you took advice from someone who's read too many quotes on the Internet. I have no idea what I'm talking about."

She laughs. "I think you do.

"I love you! Give Cade a hug for me. You know, you took that a lot better than I thought you would. You didn't freak out or anything."

"Honey, when you live through the shit I have, nothing is that shocking. Not to mention, I've known you after it happened. You are doing great, honey. If I knew you to be neurotic or angry, I might be concerned you need help. But you're good! I love you, too! I might be making a visit up to see Irma, Melody, and the baby soon."

"Let me know when and we'll do something."

With that, we disconnect the call. Feeling a little better, I decide to text Justin. Honesty is what I need to try with him. I open our text conversation. *"This is going to be a long text. I could never say any of this looking into your amazing eyes. You cast a spell on me when I look at you. Anyway, what I need to say is I'm terrified of what I told you. I think you are freaking out and you want nothing else to do with me."*

When I finish typing, I don't even go back over it to make sure it makes sense. If I do that, I'll talk myself out of sending it. I click send instantly after I finish. The feeling I have now is not as much apprehension as it is predestination. If he writes me back, it will be a goodbye. I know this, and I'm okay with it. I lay back on the bed and tuck my phone under my pillow. I close my eyes and attempt to get some desperately needed sleep to reset my brain. Emotions are totally useless.

৪০ ৫৪ ৪০ ৫৪ ৪০ ৫৪ ৫৪ ৪০ ৫৪ ৪০ ৫৪

When the afternoon sun is starting to warm up my room, Kate comes in with coffee. "Wake up! I made you coffee. Get up and hang out with me."

I smile and turn my face into the pillow. "I can't believe I actually fell asleep. What are we eating?"

"Get your ass up and let's talk about it," she starts. "We need to go to the store."

Sitting up, I take the coffee from her and drink it. "Mmmm, thanks so much. This is amazing. Let me put some clothes on and we can go. I assume we're going for full-out funky today?"

"You assume correctly. We are going to be as funky as possible because we have no one to impress."

I take another drink of coffee. "And I assume we are also going for full-on junk mode with food?"

"Abso-fucking-lutely," she answers smugly.

I nod. "Fair enough. I'll be out in ten minutes."

Curiosity is killing me. I need to know if Justin responded. I take a deep breath before looking at the screen. The plan is to do this like a Band-aid; rip it off quick. I'm pleasantly surprised he responded. I unlock my phone and pull up messages.

His response is simple, *"I'm glad you trusted me. I'm freaked out, but not for the reasons you think. Can I see you tonight?"*

Unsure of what to say, I decide I'll deal with him later. Today is about spending time with Kate and getting our heads together. She needs this more than I do. I put my hair up in a messy bun, throw on some yoga pants, flip flops, and a T-shirt.

On my way out of my room, I grab a black hoodie. Kate is waiting on the couch, dressed as my twin. We both laugh, and congratulate each other on the bun game we are both rocking.

"Bun game bigger than your future," she says sarcastically.

"You know this," I agree.

Kate drives and we raid the grocery store like a couple of teenagers. We settle on a Crockpot of rotel dip, chicken nuggets, macaroni & cheese, and some chips. We also swing through the frozen section and pick out a quart of ice cream for each of us. I grab some Rocky Road, she opts for Neapolitan. All set to gain fifteen pounds today, we check out, and go home. We pick a chick movie on Netflix and sit back with our pile of junk.

Halfway through the movie, my phone vibrates. I check and its Justin texting again. *"Are you okay?"*

Puzzled, I text him back. *"I'm okay. Why?"*

"You didn't reply to my last text, and I wanted to know you were good. So I guess that means you don't want to keep working on this."

"I never said that. I took a sick day from work to help Kate with something."

"Are you saying we can work on it?"

"Of course we can," I answer. *"You know the worst there is to know about me."*

His answer nearly sends me into a tailspin. *"And it's not so bad. Can I see you later tonight?"* I can't focus on anything after I read it.

I sigh and smile at the phone. I'm nodding to myself when Kate notices I'm distracted and she pauses the movie. "Do you need to take that?"

Busted. "No. Sorry. I'm good. It was Justin again."

"Wooooo, luva boi," she whines.

I grin and blush at the same time as I text him back. "*Tomorrow night at seven.*"

"Woah, that blush. You told him!" she exclaims.

I nod. "I did."

"And!" she exclaims as she jumps to the edge of her seat.

I shrug. "And nothing. He was kind of in shock when I last saw him. He didn't say anything. I thought for sure this whole thing was over. But apparently not. He wants to see me tonight."

Kate is a sight to behold as she sits cross-legged on the couch bouncing up and down. "Do it, jerkface."

"Jerkface? Really? I call in sick when I'm trying to get promoted, and you call me a jerkface! I don't know about doing it, but I'll see him tomorrow night. Tonight is all about us!"

She laughs and plays the movie. I watch in awe. It's based on a bestselling romance series, and oh, my God, is it hot. This might be one of my new favorites. Kate is doing nothing but making fun of the serious, sexy faces the guy keeps making.

She has a point, it is hysterical! He looks on the verge of constipation. Not quite the look the director wanted, I'm sure. Still, when he put his hands on that woman, I feel like I have tunnel vision. *It's been way too long*

7 - Assent

I never thought this week would end! It has been quite the rollercoaster. I've been in the clouds one minute, and in the gutter the next. Someone who doesn't know me might think I was manic. I'm excited to see Justin tonight. He's coming to my place since Kate has practice and setup for their bout tomorrow night. It's a once a month thing, so everyone is required to help out.

Dee still hasn't made her hiring decision, but I got a chance to size up my competition. Her resume was left on the printer. She's my age, but she has a bachelor's degree from U of M. My degree is just an Associates. She's been working in the field for a development company her uncle owns. It seems a little silly to note that your uncle owns the company you work for on your resume.

I'm trying to break into development. My self-confidence is shaken, I can't lie. I'm intimidated. I keep my nose to the grindstone, and try to keep the Dragon Lady happy. Looks like I may be with her a while longer. The thought is depressing.

Several times throughout the day I think the clock has broken. It has been an uphill battle reaching the end. I end up leaving fifteen minutes earlier than I normally do.

Friday's are more relaxed around the office, and I'm actually excited about tonight. Dare I hope that this could be something? Something real.

While I'm driving home, all I can do is think about that night at the bar. My nerves are crawling under my skin in the most delicious way as I think about how he kissed me. How his hand explored my body. His skill evident by the way he'd made me feel exquisite.

I had felt beautiful, confident, and safe. Part of me can't help but wonder how different it will be now that he knows. Does he even still want me? Tonight may be the end for us. The thought is chilling and depressing at the same time.

At home, I do a quick clean up. I start the dishwasher, wipe down all the counters, tidy the living room, and turn on my fragranced wax burner. Cinnamon puts me in the mood for the upcoming holidays. Plus, it smells like baking. I laugh when I remember the movie *Clueless*. It was one of her tips for seducing a boy: put something in the oven so it smells like you're baking. They love it! Oh, the things I think of at all the wrong times. When I finish cleaning the bathroom and making my bed, I hop in the shower.

After I blow-dry my hair, I dress in a long-sleeve, black T-shirt and a black maxi skirt. I don't bother with shoes or makeup. He gets the full, real me tonight. I finish getting ready by clipping a long piece of my asymmetrical hair style back with a barrette. I look like a flashback to the nineties, and I enjoy the way that makes me feel.

I stare in the full-length mirror a little longer than necessary. The outfit I've chosen actually makes me look taller. Perhaps it's just the weight of everything being lifted from my shoulders, but I think I even look stronger.

I'm startled when the doorbell rings. Fortifying my resolve, I answer to find Justin standing there in that leather jacket and trademark beanie. "Hi," I say in greeting.

His smile is all I need to kill the nerves in my chest. "Hi," he replies.

I return his smile with a timid one of my own. "Won't you come in?" I stand back to allow him through the door.

"Don't mind if I do. I brought a gift," he says as he holds out a brown paper bag to me.

I take it and open the bag and take out the bottle of Sauvignon Blanc. "Thank you. This is actually my favorite kind of wine. Would you care for a glass?"

He nods. "I would, but first..." He steps closer to me, wrapping his arm around my waist. He pulls me closer to him and leans down, ever so cautiously. I push up on my toes to help close the distance. When we're sharing our breaths, but not quite touching lips, he whispers, "Is this okay?"

My answer is breathless, "Yes."

In that same moment, he kisses me. It's tender and soft. He's still asking permission with his lips. I can't blame him because I'm the one that freaked out. I answer his unspoken question by sliding the tip of my tongue over his bottom lip. His lips part even more as he deepens the kiss. His other arm drops around my neck so he's now wrapped around me from head to waist. All I can do is lean into him as I'm still holding the wine and can't find any other way to steady myself as my knees weaken. His tongue caresses mine as we continue to build intensity and, at the same time, trust between us as we kiss.

He breaks from my mouth and rests his face in the crook of my neck. He breathes me in, and says, "God. I didn't realize how much I could miss you in just a few days."

The smile across my face is genuine. That kind of statement makes me happy. I bury my face in his jacket and say, "I know what you mean. How about that wine?"

"If you think that's a good idea."

I nod and pull against his arms. "I do. Have a seat. I'll get some glasses." When I try to step away from him, my knee buckles a little and I stumble.

He catches and steadies me. "Have you been drinking already?"

Feigning offense, I say, "Uh no. I don't drink *all* the time." I say as I make my way into the kitchen.

He unleashes that gorgeous laugh. "Yeah you do. I haven't been around a non-drinking Alana yet."

"True story," I answer his taunting as I pull two stemless wineglasses from the cabinet over the sink. Returning to the living room I find him settled on the couch, no jacket, and smiling from ear to ear. "You'll need to check that smile if you want to get through tonight."

"Why's that?"

"Because there's a lot of ground to cover, and I can't focus when you smile like that."

He takes the corkscrew, wine, and glasses from me. Acting as my bartender again, he opens the wine and pouring a glass for each of us. "Maybe we don't need to focus right now. There'll be time for that. The biggest thing you need to know is I don't plan on running for the hills."

His words surprise me. I take a sip of wine. "Good to know."

He smiles and says, "I know I freaked a little bit the other night. It wasn't you; you need to know that."

I agree and keep drinking. "Also good to know." I give him a shy smile. "If it wasn't me, was it you?"

He laughs. "Sort of. We can talk about it later."

I frown. "I think I'd like to talk about it now. What happened to you for two days?"

He's shifty when he answers, "I had some research to do. Called a friend of mine from back home to help out."

"What? Why?" My mind spins as I start to become paranoid. "Who are you researching?"

"We'll talk about it. I promise. I don't want to talk about it right now. What I want is to enjoy an evening with you before we do. There'll be plenty of time for us to talk through all of that." He slides closer to me and takes my wine out of my hand. Setting it on the table, he shifts to face me, staring into my eyes.

After a moment, he kisses me again. I can't help the way I fall into him. I feel like I'm sliding down a spiral slide as I kiss him back. He works a magic spell on me that I'm powerless against. It's like breathing air for the first time, or stepping out into a spring day after a long winter—he's refreshing and warming. I continue to fall. When we're starved for air, he breaks the kiss and rests his forehead on mine. "Are you still okay with this? I don't want to push you," he whispers.

Standing, I hold my hand out to him. He hesitates before taking it. I lead him into my bedroom, and turn to lock the closed door behind us.

He clears his throat as he sits on the end of the bed. "You sure?"

I walk toward him as I nod. "Yep, but one thing," I say. "This is not a commitment. It's just...a thing. You know what I mean?"

"No strings. Understood."

I step between his legs, invading his personal space. "Exactly. Not that I don't want strings, but..."

Justin places his hands on my hips and looks up at me. "I know you've been through some really hard shit in your life. So you don't want strings in case things get tough. I want you to know I'm not going anywhere. No matter what. I have my own condition, though."

"Okay, what is it?" I ask.

He moves his hands up to my face, holding me in place so I'm forced to look in his eyes. Those achingly deep, knowing brown eyes. "You can't run either. Don't shut me out," he says. "No matter what."

I start to argue, but the energy rolling off of him makes me too weak to form that thought. "Okay," I say.

"Okay," he answers. "You know how you said I work a spell on you?"

"You do."

"You have had me mesmerized since I laid eyes on you. You are all I can think about. I don't want to scare you, but I haven't been able to close my eyes without seeing you hovering over me that one night."

Closing my eyes, I shake my head. "I know what you mean."

Standing, he pulls me to him in a tight embrace. Lowering his hands, he slides them over the curve of my hips down to my ass. I press my body into his as close as I possibly can. He's kissing my neck and tugging on my earlobe with his mouth as his hands move back to my hips, then toward my stomach.

Moving my shirt out of the way, and finding the waistband of my skirt, he slides it down inch by inch. Once past my hips, it drops to the floor in a pool around my feet. I step out and kick it behind me. Standing before him in my underwear and a T-shirt, I'm all too aware of the sexual tension transitioning into anxiety.

I'm scared to let him see the scar again. *Again*. He's seen it once already and he wasn't scared of it. I take a deep breath as he slides my shirt up, just as slowly as when he removed my skirt. I close my eyes and swallow hard.

My shirt inches closer to my face, and I stand stock-still as he lifts it off over my head. My nerves get the better of me, and I start to shake. He wraps his arms around me, preventing me from moving away from him. Then he makes soothing sounds, "Shhh. I've got you. We don't have to do anything."

It's almost alien when I hear myself say, "I want to; don't stop."

He begins to kiss me from that tiny, tender place behind my ear, down my jawline to my neck. I have to steady myself by holding on to his waist. His hands explore every inch of my body from shoulders to hips. He kisses trails between my breasts down to my bellybutton. When he reaches my stomach, he kisses a path toward the scar. With a hand on the scar on my back, he kisses the scar on my stomach. My anxiety begins to ease when he says, "This wasn't your fault." He kisses the scar over and over again. Between each one he says, "You're amazing. You're a survivor. You're a fighter. You're beautiful." Each phrase makes me cry a bit more. Not tears of anxiety or pain, but tears of relief. As if I've been forgiven for something I had no control over.

I can't resist any longer, and I tangle my fingers in his hair as I tug him away from my scar and back to my mouth. Salty tears fall on to our lips as I kiss him. He wipes my tears and saying, "Don't cry."

I help him out of his clothes as he finishes removing mine. Kissing him might be my new favorite thing to do. I only stop long enough to crawl on to the bed with him. I'm desperate for him. Desperate to correct that night when I lost my mind and ruined everything. When he wraps himself around me, I push him over so I can be on top. He adjusts so he's posed to enter me. I kiss him, shifting my hips against him, and he responds by pushing into me. He makes me feel overly full, and causes an ache deep down. It's an ache I haven't felt in a very long time. He knows and allows me a moment to adjust to the feeling before starting to move.

He keeps his hands on my hips to steady me as he does. I'm lost in sensation. I moan with every movement. Sitting up to change the angle, his mouth captures my right nipple. He tugs, and a delicious searing ripple of pleasure moves through me. My back arches as a tightening builds deep down. Justin unleashes a delicious torture by moving to my left nipple.

I hold his mouth to me by pulling on his hair. The tighter I hold, the more he thrusts his hips. He moves his hands from my hips to my waist, and then he rolls us so he's on top of me. It all becomes too much as he repeatedly presses into me, and I cry out as an orgasm rips me apart. Soon, Justin follows me over the edge.

He's kissing me when he does, and I take all of his pleasure. It fills me in all the broken and cracked places, connecting us in a more intimate way than I thought possible. He stills and rests between my legs with his head on my chest. I just hold him until the shaking between us subsides.

Neither of us wants to break the moment, but he shifts to spoon me from behind. His body heat is suffocating, and my mind is a jumbled mess. I want to move, but I'm afraid to let go.

8 - Connection

The next morning I wake up freezing. Stretching, I wave my hand around on the bed looking for Justin. I come up empty-handed. The thought that he left before I woke up is upsetting. I sit straight up and look around the room as if he will magically appear if I do. Frustrated, I get up to pee and he's not in the bathroom either. I throw on an old sweatshirt and some boxer shorts. As I tie my hair up into a bun, I walk to the kitchen. The smell of coffee is calling to me. I'm startled when I make it to the kitchen because it's not Kate making breakfast. It's Justin. A shirtless Justin.

For some reason, I can't force my feet to move forward, and my arms are stuck in my hair as if I can no longer remember how to tie the rubber band. My mouth dries when he turns and says, "Good morning." I want to return his happy greeting, but I can't. He seems to realize I'm locked up because he sets down the bacon skillet, and pads over to me. He kisses me and whispers a repeated, "Good morning," against my lips.

"Mmm-morning," I stammer.

He smiles and returns to his duties in the kitchen. I take a seat at the breakfast bar and watch him work. When I gather my wits, I ask, "Did you sleep well?"

"I did. Better than I have in a long time. How about you?"

"Great."

He looks at me over his left shoulder. "Sarcasm? This early?"

I shrug. "I don't know how to do this."

Turning fully to face me, he asks, "Do what?"

Waving my hands around the kitchen, but mainly at him. "This. The morning after. I've never...I don't know."

"Feeling awkward?"

I nod.

"Why? I've seen you in the throes of pleasure, so you would think breakfast would be no big deal after that."

I groan and put my head down on folded arms across the counter. "See! That!"

He laughs, "Calm down. It's no big deal. No ties, remember?"

"I know. But...what if Kate... Where is she anyway?" I stand and locate my purse to try and put hands on my phone. It takes a few minutes, but I find it and I don't have any texts, missed calls, or messages.

Concerned, Justin comes to stand behind me. "Everything okay?"

"No. She didn't call or text. And she didn't come home. She usually lets me know where she's gonna be. This is weird."

"Hmmm, let me check my phone." He retrieves his phone from his jacket from the couch. As he walks back to me he says, "Everything is fine. Cameron met up with her last night and they are at my place."

"Oh! Thank God," I say, relieved. "Wait! Is that a good thing? Is Cameron a gentleman?"

Justin chuckles. "You met him, right? He's a guy, and she's gorgeous. I'm sure he treated her well, but you know what's up." He winks.

I ponder it for a moment. "Yeah, I know what's up, but he wouldn't hurt her would he?"

"Of course not!" he answers quickly.

Justin finishes making me eggs, bacon, pancakes, and coffee. For some reason, I'm ravenous this morning, and I don't even enjoy small talk over breakfast. No, I shovel it in like there's no tomorrow. I think at one point I expressed my appreciation by gurgling, "Mmm, this is amazing," between bites. When I'm nearly done with my food, I sit back to breathe, and I notice he's watching me.

"Enthusiastic, aren't ya?" he observes.

"Shut up. It's your fault. Wore me out last night. I need to replenish my strength."

His look is all-consuming when he says, "Please let me know when you're ready for me to ravage you again."

I nearly choke on my coffee. "Uh, will do. So what do you have planned for today?"

He shrugs. "I left my weekend wide open. You decide."

I gape. "You mean we have the whole weekend together?"

"If that's what you want. Of course, if you want to send me packing, you can do that, too."

I think it over and decide I really like the idea of actually getting to know him. "Let's do something fun. You decide what we do with the day, and I'll decide what we do tonight."

His face seems perplexed, but very much onboard with this deal. "Okay. What do you have in mind for tonight?"

Grinning ear-to-ear, I lean forward and tell him about Kate's roller derby bout and suggest we go. "It's hella fun! Plus, they have beer and food trucks."

He thinks for a moment, and it takes him so long I start to think he's not okay with this idea. Finally, he says, "Okay a night of beer and debauchery it is. So for the day, we do something outdoors to earn our beer and nachos."

"Keep talking. What do you have in mind?"

"We're going to Cameron's family cabin near Jackson. They have land, and I can show you the trails we used to hike when we were growing up."

It sounds amazing. The win is spending the day with Justin. Maybe he'll tell me why he's not a cop anymore. I mean, I didn't even know you could quit that profession. I've always thought it was the kind of career that ran in your blood. Once a cop, always a cop, right? Not knowing that bugs me.

"It's a date. First up, showers!"

ଚୀଓଞ୍ଚୀଓଞ୍ଚୀଓଞ୍ଚୀଓଞ୍ଚୀଓଞ

A couple hours later, we're parking his truck in front of the cabin. It's tiny; probably only a one bedroom and one bathroom. We packed a cooler with some lunch and drinks because Justin wasn't sure if Cameron or his parents have the cabin stocked right now. Justin pulls the key out of fake rock and opens the door. I didn't initially notice the rock because it was under a bush by the front steps. After the ride, we decide to start by relaxing and catching our breath.

Justin sits on the couch with one leg up and one leg on the floor. I slide my jacket off and take a seat between his legs. Laying my head on his chest, he wraps his arms around me then kisses me on the head. I close my eyes and just enjoy the moment. Sitting in the silence with him is so necessary. I can start to appreciate the rhythm of his breathing and the timing of his heartbeat. My brain notes how his heartbeat coincides with my own. Not on the same timing, but complimentary.

I think he starts to notice, too. Before we get so settled we forget about our hike, he says, "All right. Time to go. We'll stay here forever if we don't move." I agree with him because the longer we sit here like this, the more I think about what else we could be doing. Amazing things—that's what we could be doing.

We both stand, put on our jackets, and then walk out the front door. He reaches for my hand as we descend the front steps. Hiking into the woods right by the driveway, we make it two hundred yards away when he says, "So, what is it you want to know?"

I clear my throat. "Why aren't you a cop anymore?"

"Wow. You get right to it, don't you? Being a cop was the only thing I ever wanted to do with my life. I was the one who did all the research and figured out how I could get both of us into the academy. Dude, we worked so hard. Cameron was always a thin kid, but he was never very athletic. We had to work hard and train every day so he could pass the physical part of the academy. The good thing was that we balanced each other, as we had for our whole lives. I could help him train he helped me study. Kid is a genius. Anyway, there was a situation. It affected me. There wasn't anything I could do, and I couldn't let it go. It eats, er, *ate* me alive. I quit when it became too much for me."

"What was it?"

He stops walking and takes both of my hands in his. "I'm not sure I'm ready to tell you," he says quietly.

This makes me defensive. "I told you my story. It took a piece of my soul to do that. Is it worse than what I lived through?"

He shakes his head. "No. But I don't think you'll find it coincidental either."

Furrowing my brow, I ask, "What are you talking about?" My blood pressure is rising as my heartbeat picks up. It's a pounding in my ears. *"Don't panic. Hear him out. See what he means."*

He leads me to a large rock in the clearing nearby and asks me to sit. He sighs and begins, "I've been debating whether or not to tell you any of this. I can see, now, you need to know. It's a roadblock we have to hurdle. You trusted me, so I'm going to trust you. Let me finish telling you the story before you ask any questions, okay?"

I nod.

He starts to pace as he pulls his thoughts together. "So one night, I was off work and my buddy was having a poker night at his place. Dude was a total, cliché bachelor. He had a rundown trailer in the middle of nowhere. We played until well past midnight, and I was bit buzzed when we wrapped up. I was broke from losing all my money. I was anxious to get home, and fall in the bed. On my way home, I see a person stumble from the woods out on to the road. I have to swerve to miss them. I mean just came walking straight toward the truck with no regard for their own life. Waving one hand in the air and walking directly at me. I had to jump on brakes, and the wheels locked up, squealing as I stopped."

He looks at me, and studies my reaction before continuing. My heart continues to race, and despite the panic welling up in my brain as I'm piecing this together, I remain quiet.

"I jump out of the truck, ready to rip into the guy's ass for being so dumb. I'm in cop mode even though I'm off-duty. I went to the back of the truck, only when I do, the guy is gone. Right then I notice that the passenger door of the truck is open, and the guy has gotten inside. I run up and grab the door, only to see the person inside my truck is..."

This is it. The blood in my veins is cold. I know what comes next, but I need him to say it.

Justin stops pacing and squats in front of me, holding my hands. "... Is a woman. She's bleeding a ton, and holding her stomach. Then she says 'please help me.' I lift the edge of her soaked shirt and see that she's been shot. There's a gaping wound right next to her hip."

Tears are pooling my eyes as he's talking. I was that woman in his truck. He's describing what happened to me. He's retelling my nightmare.

"I pulled off my flannel shirt and wadded it up under her hand to help staunch some of the bleeding. I drove like a maniac to get her to the hospital. I kept asking her who did this to her, but she was passed out cold. The only sounds she made when she would surface into consciousness were groans of pain or deep sobs. I used my cell to call a friend of mine who's a nurse in the ER.

"She had a team and a gurney at the ambulance drop off door when I pulled up. They scooped the woman out of my truck and rolled her away. My friend, Marcy, told me I reeked of beer and I needed to go home before my sergeant showed up to start the investigation."

Justin reaches up and wipes hot tears from my cheeks. I'm numb. I can barely tell I'm still sitting. My breathing is shallow as I try to fight the urge to run away from him.

"I didn't want to leave. I was going to come back and help investigate what happened to that woman. To me, it was clearly a domestic issue. You see, my mother died when I was a teenager. My stepfather was an abusive asshole, and she refused to leave. She always covered for him and made excuses. I knew the signs. I knew when I checked her wound. I knew because I saw all the bruises on her body. Her face was swollen across her cheeks. I know the signs of a backhand to the face."

Sobs wrack my body. This can't be real. I can't even look at him.

"The next day, I called my sergeant to ask to be assigned to the case. He declined my request because of my background. He knew it was domestic, too. So, I went on my own to see if Marcy would help me find her so I could talk to her. Marcy tried, but you were gone."

When he says, *"You were gone,"* I snap and look at him. "What do you mean, I was gone?"

He rubs his thumbs in circles over the backs of my hands as he holds them, "I think you know what I mean."

Everything has clicked into place. It all adds up. The safe feeling I have with him. I do know what he means, but my mind can't comprehend how. *How is it that Justin was there that night? Why was it him?* Something he said about coincidence comes back to my mind and I mumble, "No, I guess it wasn't a coincidence, was it?"

He's quiet when he asks, "Baby? Are you okay? What can I do?"

Tears are still flowing down my cheeks, and I all I can do is shake my head. The word is barely audible when I say, "Nothing."

"Please," he begs, "let me do something to help. I can't stand to see you like this."

I sit frozen as I process what he's just told me. I think through what he's asking of me. *What is it I need? How can he help me? Can I be helped?* I've been alone with this secret for five years. I had to change my appearance and my identity. What I gave up I can never get back. I lost my child, my parents, my friends, and my life. Justin didn't do this; Kent did. He stole my youth, my child, and my life.

Will I let him steal this, too? As that realization dawns on me, I reach for Justin, and grab a handful of his jacket. I pull him to me, and he obliges by placing both knees fully on the ground where he's been slightly kneeling. As he moves closer, I let go of his jacket and slide my hands around his shoulders and hold him to me. I squeeze him and crack wide open. Relief, heartache, memories, who I was, who I am, and who I will be collide in my shattered heart.

Justin doesn't say anything else, he just holds me until the sun begins to set and the tears subside. I'm not even sure I'm done crying, but I'm out of tears. My breathing is hitching, and I'm hiccupping as I try to find a way to settle down. In this one week, I have re-lived the worst moment of my life too many times. More than I have in the last five years.

Together, we stand to head back to the cabin. Justin wraps me in his arms, and I lean on him to try and make the walk back. My body feels like it's been through a hurricane, a tornado, or hit by a truck. Every step is a chore.

When we reach the cabin, I sit numbly on the couch and Justin starts a fire. He pours us both a drink from the family stash in the kitchen and comes to sit with me. Robotically, I take a long drink. It burns and tingles in my arms all the way to my fingers. I take another drink and the tingles move into my feet. When the alcohol has the desired effect by calming me, I start asking questions.

"Is this what you were researching when you went off the grid?"

"Yes. Sort of. I was doing a background check on Kent."

"Why did you tell me? You could have kept it to yourself. I wouldn't have ever known."

"You asked me why I'm not a cop anymore. It's one of the biggest contributing factors," he answers. "You wouldn't have known it was me if I didn't tell you, but I would know."

"Why would what happened to me make you quit?"

He sighs deeply and says, "Because I couldn't help you. Because what happened to you was very close to how I lost my mom. It was something I'd never fully dealt with, and here it was happening to someone else. Being a cop was supposed to allow me to help people, and I failed."

"But you did help me. I wouldn't be here right now if you hadn't gotten me to the hospital. Did you forget that part?"

"I know. But I couldn't find and punish the man that did that to you. I did investigations on my own. I went out, and visited every trailer and house in the area of where I picked you up. No one could identify a missing woman with brown hair. There was one guy I thought was suspicious, but when I ran his record, there was nothing out of line. I hit a wall. No leads. Nothing. I failed."

I shake my head. "You met Kent."

"I did, and he was as you said. Charming. Charismatic. A smooth talker. It made me even more suspicious of him. "Can I ask you something else?"

I nod.

"How did you disappear?"

His question takes me by surprise. It's another part of my life I haven't told anyone. This one I've never even told Irma. She never asked, and I wasn't keen on sharing. I take a few minutes to drum up those memories. That time when I wasn't who I am comes flooding back with all of the fear of surviving.

"When I woke up after surgery, I realized where I was and that the hospital was still too close to Kent. As my head cleared from the anesthesia, I started to freak. I started to think that at any moment, Kent would show up and claim me. The nurse tending to me was kind. She kept asking my name, but I wouldn't tell her. I think I was in shock. It wasn't that I couldn't speak, I didn't know what to say, and I didn't want to talk to anyone. The humiliation of the whole ordeal still haunts me, but I've learned to cope with it."

"That afternoon, when the nurse finished changing my IV bag, I decided I needed to disappear. As I figured, I had two choices: one would be to recover in the hospital, go through an investigation with the police, and go through some ugly domestic violence case if they could help. My other option was to die. I decided to let Kent think I had.

"On one of her visits to check vitals, the nurse told me the new nurse for the next shift would be around to meet me in a few minutes. People are sloppy during shift changes, in all professions. I took advantage of the opportunity to slip out. It took every ounce of strength I had to pull myself out of the bed without falling."

He wraps his arms around me and squeezes me close to his side. I heave a deep breath. The weight of recalling those moments is almost unbearable.

"Eventually, I felt steady enough to walk out into the hallway. Everyone was busy with phones, carts, and buzzing around in and out of the other rooms. I continued down the hall to a room marked staff. Inside that room, I found a drawer that had extra scrubs for the nurses. They weren't my size, but they weren't too terribly big. When I was dressed, I went to the elevator at the end of the hallway and left."

"In the back of the building, there was a convenient store near the parking lot. There, I found a truck driver who was making a snack cake delivery. When he came out, I was standing next to a car, and I sold him a sob story about my car being broken down. He had mercy on me and drove me to his next stop, which was in a town where I had convinced him I had family. From that town, I found a ride with another delivery driver, and so on. One after another they helped me, until I found Jayne. She was a clerk at the convenient store in Bell Hills. She didn't buy my broken down car story. Her powers of observation noted that my scrubs were from the hospital one hundred miles away."

Justin rubs my arms rhythmically to soothe me as I continue.

"I cried. Exhaustion had gotten the best of me, and the pain from the gunshot and surgery was building. I told her I left the hospital without being released. That I had surgery and needed a place to rest for the night and to change the dressing on my wound. She didn't ask any questions. She had me rest in the back office until her shift was over.

"When we left the store, she took me for some dinner and then to a shelter. There I met Lisa, who ran a shelter for abused and homeless women. Again, there were no questions. I would come to learn that Lisa had helped Jayne out of a bad time. Lisa gave me a place to live, and acted as a counselor as I recuperated. The town doctor came to the shelter to check on my recovery as well as the other women's medical needs. Eventually, she helped me by giving me a job in the shelter. Over time, as I got back on my feet, I was able to get a job outside of the shelter."

"Jayne, Lisa, and I spent a lot of time together that first year. Lisa introduced me to a friend of hers who could provide me a new identity. She knew I couldn't go back to Kent, and I didn't stand a chance of proving anything. Well, that's what we were both convinced of, anyway. We worked together to color my hair and come up with a story about who I am. Stan, her friend, did all the paperwork and pictures. A few weeks later, I became Alana. I've been her ever since."

After a few minutes of processing, he says, "What happened to your son?"

I shrug. "I don't know. I've taken comfort all this time in that Kent was crazy in love with him. Ethan is his legacy, and I don't think he would ever lay a hand on him. Kent hated me, so I think with me out of the way, he might be happier. I know how crazy that sounds. Like I was a catalyst for his insanity."

He agrees, "You can't blame yourself. No one deserves to be treated that way, ever."

Still drinking whatever Justin poured for us, I feel even calmer and like the panic is dissipating. Standing, I walk to the windows at the back of the cabin. They overlook a large expanse of land. I was never good at estimating acres or anything like that, so I can't wrap my mind around how much land I'm looking at. In the sky, the stars are like spotlights. Bright and beautiful, it's as if they have each been assigned a tree of their own. There are even some stars that cover the small pond. For a cold night, the sky is ridiculously clear. It's like watching HDTV through a window. Only, it's real. I use my observations of my surroundings a way to center my thoughts and ground myself.

Justin is cautious as he approaches me, sliding his arms around my waist from behind. I relax into him and we take in the scenery together. After a long silence between us, he whispers in my ear, "That's enough for tonight. It's late. We'll stay here instead of heading back. How are you feeling?"

I turn in his arms, look up into his eyes, and pull back from his embrace. I have to do this now, and I need a little space between us. "I need to tell you something else. I didn't want to tell you, but..."

"You can tell me anything. What is it?" he asks, concerned.

"This week when I left work sick, I wasn't sick."

He looks puzzled. "Okay. Go on."

I sigh, "I was taking lunch alone to get my head together about us. When I heard an unmistakable voice. It was so clear to me who it was. I locked up right there on the sidewalk. Eventually, I looked around the corner, and it was Kent. He was downtown at one of the buildings near mine. I had a panic attack and ran home."

His ears start to turn red. *That must be his tell.* When he formulates a thought, it isn't what I expect. "It's okay. You did good to go home and take yourself out of the situation and harm's way. Don't worry about. I'll take care of it."

"Please don't do anything. He didn't see me. He can't be looking for me."

He nods, "Okay. Why don't you go get a bath, and I'll see what's in the cabinets for dinner. I can't promise high-end cuisine, but we won't go hungry."

I relax as I step back towards him, and he wraps his arms around me. I slip my arms around his neck, raising on tiptoes to kiss him. "Thank you."

ဆဝങဆဝങဆဝങဆဝങဆဝങဝങ

In the bathroom, I dig around and find everything I need. It would seem there is at least one woman in Cameron's family. She keeps some pretty good bath salts, hair products, and plush towels. I also find a nice thick robe. I start the water to let it warm up and then add some bath salts after I put the stopper down.

Undressing, I stare at myself in the mirror. I'm a stranger. It's like I'm seeing my face for the first time since that night. Turning from side to side, I check myself over from head to toe. My hand involuntarily covers my scar. It's the one thing about that night I can't get rid of, or keep hidden. It will always remind me. No matter what it tells me about myself, I know one thing to be true: I survived.

Sliding into the hot bath, I realize I've run it way too hot. My skin pinks on contact. The sting is what I need to feel alive and relax my overly tense muscles. Tonight has been plain exhausting. I sink all the way down and let the water cover as much of my skin as possible. When the water starts to cool, I sit up and hug my knees to my chest. Justin knocks on the door.

"Come in," I call.

Slowly, Justin opens the door, and asks, "Is this okay?"

I nod and he enters the bathroom. He takes a seat on the edge of the tub and strokes my frizzy, humid-laden hair from my face.

"Want to hold me a few minutes?" I ask.

"Yeah, I do. I need to hold you," he says with a hint of genuine desperation in his voice. A quality I've not heard in him before.

I scooch forward in the tub until my knees are against the side with the faucet. While he undresses, I let some of the cooling water out so that I can run more hot water for us to share. He sits behind me, placing his legs on either side of me. Once he's settled, I slide back until my back is against his front. I lay my head back on his shoulder. It only takes a split second for his arms to wrap me in a firm embrace, holding me to him. We indulge in our intimacy without a word. He rubs my arms, and I run my hands over his legs. He kisses the top of my head, and I take comfort in him. More than anything, we hold on to each other. He makes everything better.

ༀ༄ༀ༄ༀ༄ༀ༄ༀ༄ༀ༄

The dinner Justin managed to put together for us was frozen chicken nuggets that he cooked in the oven and a bucket of macaroni and cheese that could feed a small army of kindergarteners. We eat our fill, dressed in bathrobes in front of the fireplace.

"Quite frankly, sir, that might be the best mac and cheese I've ever eaten," I say.

His glorious smile is back. "You only think that because you're starving to death."

"I'm not. Not anymore. I ate the world's most magical mac and cheese, so I'm good now."

He laughs. "World's most magical? That's a new one."

"Yep. It's a new level of awesome. What do we do now? I think it's probably too late to make the drive back and still make the roller derby bout."

He reaches over to dab some cheese off the corner of my mouth. "How about we start by finishing dinner and going to bed. Tomorrow will have its own share of trouble, and tonight, I need to hold you and sleep. It feels like I've been hit by a truck, and I'm sure you aren't feeling too great."

He's right, of course, so we do exactly as he suggested. We finish eating, wash the dishes, and lock up the cabin. He removes my robe and tucks me into bed as if I'm precious to him. He climbs into bed behind me and wraps himself around me in a spoon fashion. I've never felt this content and safe in all of my life. The feeling is overwhelming. Eventually, I'm able to fall asleep and enjoy the warmth and stability Justin provides.

9 - Attack

The morning sun rises through the window by the bed. I'm too hot and almost sweating from the heat radiating from Justin's body. He's like a space heater or electric blanket in the bed with me. I squirm to get free from his hold, but it's useless. I try to pull away, and he grumbles as he squeezes me tighter. As I lay awake, staring at the beautiful scenery from the bedroom window, our conversation plays over and over in my mind.

Justin is the man who rescued me. All those nights remembering my escape, I couldn't remember his face. It has haunted me that a stranger saved me. A mixture of emotions swirl through my mind, among them gratitude, fear, and anxiety. When I think of that night, the outstanding memory of that man is safety. He made me feel safe. This is why I felt like I knew him when we met. I do know him. I've known him for a long time. I was unaware of that fact until last night. I sigh.

"What are you thinking about?" A deep, scratchy morning voice rumbles in my ear.

I shrug. "Everything."

Justin kisses the back of my head. "I know. Me too."

"When I told you my story, about how I died and started over, is that why you freaked out? You knew when I told you that I was the woman you saved that night?"

I can feel him nod. "I suspected. There were so many similarities. What I didn't tell you was that, when I left the force, I kept looking. Your face was unrecognizable from the bruising and swelling. So I was looking for a needle in a haystack. Looking for someone with brown hair, but beyond your build and hair, I had nothing to go on. It was killing me. How strange that we would stumble across each other the way we did. That is strange, right?"

I think over this for a while, then ask, "Why did you keep looking?"

He pulls away from me and, placing a hand on my shoulder, turns me to face him. "Don't you see? I told you about my mother. I helped save you that night, but the likelihood was that you would go back to him. So many women go back over and over again until their abuser kills them. I've seen it. I knew there was more to saving you than taking you to the hospital."

"You didn't even know me. You don't know me now."

"That's not the point. After my mother was killed, I became a police officer so I could bring men like my stepfather to justice. I wanted to bury whoever did that to you or anyone else. When I didn't get assigned to the case, I became so obsessed I couldn't work any other case. It was all bullshit and didn't matter. Not to me, anyway. That's when I was brought into the captain's office and given corrective actions for not doing my job. I knew then that my passions for being a police officer, in general, were gone. Losing sight of what I had always wanted changed me. You changed me. I promise I'm not a stalker, but you brought me to Memphis. I had no idea it was you, but it *was* you. I had to broaden my search."

"When we met in the office, did you know it was me?"

"No. Five years of looking with no clues, I had basically given up. I knew you hadn't died, and that gave me comfort. But I had given up hope of ever finding you. It crushed me to admit defeat."

His answers satisfied a deep confusion I've been harboring since he told me his side of the story yesterday. I just want to bask in the safety and warmth in his arms, something I've discovered that I need. Scooting closer to him, I snuggle in to his chest, burrowing us deeper into the blankets. He tightens his hold on me in response, and I feel him let go of a breath he's been holding. I'm sure he's as scared as I am about this honesty between us.

"Why did you decide to trust me?" he asks quietly.

I shrug.

"Not good enough. Why?"

Considering what to say, I take a few minutes to answer. "Irma told me to try trusting someone."

His response is as delayed as my own. "Okay. Who's Irma?"

I smile into his chest and proceed to tell him all about my unofficial, adopted grandmother, including all of her mysterious talents. "Sounds crazy, huh?"

"That doesn't sound crazy. Every family has some friend or family member who sees things, don't they? In fact, it's kind of odd not to have someone like that around, especially in the South."

Turning my head to make eye contact with him, I reach up and feel his forehead. "You feeling okay? Sick? Fever?"

His laughter is deep and genuine. "That's not fair. You are the one who takes advice from her. You know it's not crazy."

I roll to my back and stare at the ceiling. "I owe Irma so much, taking her advice is the least I can do. She hasn't been wrong yet."

"I'd like to meet her."

"We can do that some time, I think. For now, we need to get moving if we're going to make it home this afternoon. I have a ton of stuff to do to prepare for work this week."

"Do you think we need to go right now?" he asks timidly.

I look at him. "Kind of. Why? Did you have something else we need to do here?"

His face shifts and I know exactly what he has in mind. I don't object to spending a little while longer at the cabin with him.

Dusk is a nice purplish gray as we pull into my driveway. It won't be long until full darkness. Kate's car isn't here. I idly think she must be at the grocery store or out running errands. When we approach the door, I notice it's slightly open.

Before I can say anything, Justin is nudging me aside and whispering for me to wait by the car. It takes all I have in me to do as he says. I trust that he knows what to do.

Worry makes me sick as I watch him enter the house. After a few minutes, he steps to the door and motions for me to come up the stairs. I meet him at the door, and he escorts me in.

"Is anything missing?"

I'm standing in full shock as I look around our house. It's been destroyed. Tears prick my eyes as I think of Kate. When I can make my feet move, I go straight for her room. She's not there. Justin is with me and asking again if anything is missing. I shake my head. He asks me if I think this is random. I shake my head again. Distantly, I'm aware of him calling the police to report the break in. My knees give out and I take an ungraceful seat on the floor in the middle of the living room.

Justin brings me back to the situation at hand by asking me to call Kate. I just stare at him. "Baby, you have to pull it together. Where's Kate? Can you call her?"

I nod. "Yeah. Hand me my phone."

He rummages through my purse and brings me my phone. I call Kate. It rings through to voicemail. I try again. I try many times before Justin says, "She's not answering. Would she be somewhere else? Do you know any other way of finding her?"

Slowly the fog clears and all I can say is, "The Ladies." Justin gives me an incredulous look before turning away to pace. Coughing, I clear my throat, and repeat, "The Ladies!"

Justin comes in and kneels beside me, pushing my hair from my face and wiping the tears off my cheeks. "Alana, you're not making sense. Who are The Ladies?"

I smile, and repeat myself again, "The Ladies! They're her roller derby team. That's it! We have to go find them. I know where to look. It's Sunday. Post-bout lunch and drinks! We have to go to the bar."

Still looking doubtful, Justin follows me to the car and drives me to the bar. Kate's car is in the parking lot. "She's here!" I shout as he parks. No sooner than we've stopped, I'm running into the building and Justin is trailing right behind me.

The first person I recognize is her team captain, Courtney. "Courtney! Where's Kate?"

Courtney looks surprised to see me, no doubt because we hardly know each other, but she answers, "She went home with some guy last night she's not here."

"But," I start to argue. "Her car is in the parking lot."

"Oh, yeah, my car broke down yesterday, and when she left the bout last night, she gave me her keys so I could get home."

"What? Why would she do that? Even when she's into a guy, she doesn't do that."

"Yeah, I said the same thing. She said that the guy she was leaving with is a coworker. To be honest, she didn't look that thrilled, but he was all over her. He was really into her."

I turn to look at Justin. He's still confused about what's going on, so I catch him up by way of introductions. "I'm sorry. I suck. Courtney, this is Justin, a friend of mine. Justin, this is Courtney. She's Kate's roller derby team captain. Her team is called The Derbytaints, or The Ladies for short."

He releases a breath as things start to click into place. "Nice to meet you Courtney. When was the last time you saw Kate?"

She thinks for a minute. "Probably nine or nine-thirty last night."

"Thank you. I'm going to take Alana home to wait for her."

I really don't like being told what to do, but under the circumstances, I have no choice go along with it. Kate is a sexually free spirit. It really isn't unusual for her to go home with a guy. Still, I don't like it. I wave goodbye to the girls, and we leave. Outside, Justin asks me if I know this coworker of hers.

"I don't. She's been having problems with a guy in the office. Sexual harassment. She's spoken to HR, but nothing's been done. She's creeped out hard. Really, it's scary shit. He's escalated from verbal attacks to actually putting his hands on her. You...don't think...he wouldn't," I trail off.

The look on his face must be one he reserves for authoritative situations. "I do think he would. I've seen crazier things."

"What do we do?" I ask as the panic rises up again.

"Let me make a phone call."

He apparently still has some law enforcement contacts. I'm thankful. Whoever he calls asks for Kate's description, timelines, and some other details of the condition of the house. After Justin hangs up, he says, "Now we wait."

"Wait for what?" I ask, stress filling me.

"Wait for her to be found." His calm is disturbing. He reaches out and holds my hand, pulling me closer to him in the front seat of the car.

After a few minutes that felt like an eternity, Justin's phone rings. He answers, all business. It's Cameron. He's got Kate. Justin gives nothing away as he talks to Cam. There's a lot of very stern, "uh huh", "right", and "okay." Only hearing one side of a phone conversation is nerve-wracking. Finally, he hangs up and catches me up on the information discussed on the call, and we're going to meet up with them now.

Justin is stoic as he drives. I'm begging for details and to know she's all right, but he won't answer me. He just drives. I'm too wound up to pay attention to where we're going until we're there. The hospital.

"She's hurt," I say softly.

"She's hurt," he answers an equally gentle tone.

"How?"

"Cameron didn't say. She was admitted last night and has a private room. Do you want to see her?"

I nod as I wipe tears from my face.

Justin comes around to my door, opens it, and guides me out of the car as he offers the solid support of his body. His arm around my shoulders, we walk through the parking lot. As we get closer to the doors, I decide Kate doesn't need to see me falling apart. I need to pull myself together for her, so I step away from Justin.

I straighten my top and jacket, then smooth my hair and face. "Give me a minute."

He must understand because he doesn't argue about letting me walk in on my own, slightly behind him.

We head to the fifth floor of the hospital, and it doesn't take us long to find her room where Cameron is pacing outside in the hallway. Justin shakes Cam's hand and then yanks him into a tight hug while I peer into her room. She's awake! Justin notices. "Go on inside. We'll wait here."

"You sure? You could come in with me."

"She needs you right now. I'll be here. Promise."

Kate starts crying the moment I go into the room and close the door. It would seem she's been holding it together for Cameron. I try to be gentle as I hug her. She's bruised all over her face. I can't touch her anywhere that doesn't hurt.

"God, Kate! I'm so sorry. Are you okay?"

"I think I will be," she answers coldly.

"What happened?"

She's overcome with emotion and I have to wait for it to pass before she answers me. I just hold her hand and try to be comforting. I think I'm failing miserably because she can hardly catch her breath. Finally, she tells me the guy that's been harassing her at work showed up the derby bout.

"I was assigned to work the merchandise sales table last night during the junior bout," she begins. "While I was folding some new T-shirts, he came up behind me and grabbed my ass. I jumped and turned around. When I saw who it was, I started to back away from him. Quick son-of-a-bitch made another grab for me and pulled me closer to him. Then he whispered in my ear, 'I will make a scene in front of everyone here. I know you talked to HR again. You're coming with me, right now.' He jammed something into my back that felt hard. He assured me it was what I thought it was. I thought it was a gun, but I didn't want him to lose it in there with those kids and all the people I love. So I did what he said. I called a girl over to cover the table for me real quick. She did, and I walked out with him."

"That's when you gave Courtney your keys."

She nods, wiping at her nose with a tissue. "I thought she would catch on that this was not someone I wanted to leave with. But dammit, she's no good at subtle hints."

"I know. We went looking for you at the bar, and she told us about you leaving with some guy."

"God love her, that girl is dense. Anyway..." She sniffles and I give her the whole box of tissue. "So he took me to the house. I apologized for reporting him. Just said that he had scared me and I didn't know what else to do. The look he gave me was terrifying. Like I was a piece of meat and he was about to devour me, but also there was this meanness I've never seen before."

I've seen that look.

"I told him I needed to tell you not to come home. That I was with someone. He allowed me one phone call. When he gave me the phone, I called Cameron. I was reminded that he's a former cop, ya know. I figured he was the best person to call. He could actually help. Plus, he's pretty smart. I knew if I called him and acted like he was you he'd know something was wrong. I was right. I called him and said, 'Hey Alana. I'm with someone at home tonight, can you stay with Justin?' He immediately said he was on his way over and not to hang up."

"All of that sounds like he rescued you. What went haywire?"

"He made it all right, after Kent beat my ass. Girl, he threw me against walls like a ragdoll."

I closed my eyes and let the fear seep deep into my spirit. "Kate, what's this guy's name again?"

"I never told you? His name is Kent. Kent Walsh."

10 - Security

"Oh. My. God." I get up from the chair by her bed and run out into the hallway. I blow past Justin and Cameron, headed straight for the stairwell. I don't have time for an elevator. *He found me. He found me, and he beat my roommate. He's been harassing her because of me. He. Found. Me.*

I make it down three flights of stairs before Justin catches up with me. When he does he blocks me from going down the next flight. I'm out of breath.

"Alana, what's going on?"

"I have to leave. He found me. He found Kate. He nearly killed her. He's found me and I have to leave. He'll kill me for real this time."

He's not going to kill you. Cameron and I will take care of this. Please, stop trying to run away. We don't know for sure that he's here for you. He could just be a straight-up psychopath. Please, Alana. Let me help.

"Can't breathe," I manage, barely audible.

"Come here. You can't breathe because you're having a panic attack." Justin wraps me in his arms and starts coaching me to calm me. He keeps repeating, "You're okay. You're safe. In and out. Match my breathing. Listen to my heart."

Slowly, I start to catch my breath. "What are you going to do? You aren't a cop. You can't take him out or something."

Justin looks stern. "You're right, but I know the right people. Please let Cam and I help. We can get you both protected."

Reluctantly, I agree. What choice do I have at this point? "Justin? Don't be angry with me. I'm terrified."

"I'm not. I hate that this is happening. Cameron told me who did this in the hall. When he told me, my skin went cold. I knew it would only be a split-second before Kate told you, and this would be your reaction. I should have stopped you upstairs. Girl, you can move!"

I laugh bitterly "Panic can do that to you. How did Cameron find her?"

He shakes his head. "You don't want to know. It's bad."

"I need to know. How bad?"

He thinks it over and decides to answer my question. "He beat her bad. He destroyed the house. Cameron said he thought the guy was going to rape her when he walked in and saw what was happening. She was unconscious. But that chicken-shit asshole ran from the house when Cameron busted the door in."

"I'm not surprised he's scum or a chicken-shit. It's confirmation that we're talking about the same Kent."

Justin wraps his arms around me and squeezes. "I promise this asshole will get what's coming to him. Promise. Come back upstairs and talk to the police. They'll be here any minute."

Hours later, the four of us have talked to the police. We discussed everything while waiting for them to arrive, and decided to leave out anything to do with my history with Kent. I faked my death, my son is out there somewhere, and Kent is in the wind waiting to strike again. I don't want anyone to give away my new life if I can help it at all.

Cameron decided to stay overnight with Kate. They are concerned with some internal bleeding they believe is coming from her kidneys. Thinking about how deadly Kent can be makes my blood boil. Poor, sweet Kate didn't deserve this. Her mistake was taking my advice, and it made her a target. I encouraged her to report him. How could I have known that the asshole at work was really a psychopath? How could I have known it was Kent? After all this time, he shows up here. Why? He's been looking for me after all. Is that why he was downtown that day?

My brain feels like a swirling shit storm by the time we reach my house. Justin stands guard at the door like a sentry as I move around the house packing a bag. I grab a few days' worth of work clothes, some pajamas, and some blue jeans.

It all starts to hit me again as I'm zipping my makeup bag. He's running me out of my home again. Tears prick my eyes and my hands start to shake. Justin's hands cover mine, and he takes over closing the bag. Yanking my hands back from him, I cross my arms and close my eyes, trying to regain some composure.

He's careful when he turns to face me. Slowly and gently he wraps his arms around me. I realize I don't have regain composure with Justin here. He's holding me together when it feels like the Earth has dropped out from under me. His voice is soothing as he repeats what I need to hear. *"It's not your fault. Calm down. Breathe."* I feel myself leaning into him harder as my body gives up fighting the fear and shame of this whole situation.

How could I have doubted that I wanted to have a real relationship with him? He's everything to me in this moment and has a way of comforting me like no one else can. I've been so self-reliant and terrified for so long that I was scared to let anyone else in. As I look up into his beautiful face, I know we are crossing that line between friends with benefits and something more. How much more, I'm not sure.

"Did you pack everything you need?" he asks.

I nod.

"Let's get out of here. I'm freaked out. My former sergeant made some calls; he's assigned a patrol unit to your street. None of us think Kent will come back here. He already had his fun with Kate, and he doesn't really know about you. Well, not the real you."

I shake my head. *What if he saw pictures of me while he was here with Kate.* "Justin," I start, "There are pictures of me in the house."

"There are pictures of you in the house?" he repeats.

"Yes, there's one on the fridge, one in the living room on the bookcase, and I think Kate has one of the two of us together in her room."

Before I can fully finish my sentence, Justin is in motion. "Stay here." He says it over his shoulder as he bolts from the bedroom. I do as I'm told. I can hear him rummaging around in the remnants of our things. When he comes back to me, his face is ghostly pale, and he's shaking his head.

"What is it?" I ask as the fear wells up in my throat.

"Your pictures are gone."

I take a minute to absorb what that means. Kent took the pictures. Kate wouldn't have done anything with them. He's seen my face. Do I look differently enough now that he wouldn't recognize those pictures as being the real me? "Oh, God. He knows. He'll be back for me."

"Let's go," Justin says dragging my roller bag behind him as he leaves my bedroom, clearing a way for me to follow him.

I drive my car with Justin following in his truck behind me. When we get to Justin's house, he asks me to stay in the car and lock all the doors. He doesn't want to take any chances that we've been watched recently or that we've been followed. I have a cell phone in my hand with 911 dialed, but not yet connected. I hold it for dear life as Justin inspects his house.

While I'm waiting, the thought that Kent might have put it all together is overwhelming. I can't let him hurt Kate again or even let him get close to Cam and Justin. There are too many people at stake now. What about Ethan? Where is he? Who is watching him? Kent is psychotic. He won't stop now that he knows I'm alive.

Of course, I'm only assuming, but I'm fairly certain he knows who I am. There's no way I'm going to let him hurt anyone else in my life. I have to do something, and there's only one way to stop him for good. A plan starts to form in my mind.

My thoughts have me so distracted that I'm caught off-guard when Justin returns to the car. I unlock the door. He has a gun in his hand, and he's holding it low, pointed away from us.

I've never been around guns much. Hell, the first time I can remember hearing one fired was the night I was shot. The damn things scare me to death. I keep my eye on the gun as I gather my things from the car. Justin notices. "I know how you must feel about this, but it's a necessary evil."

I nod. "I just don't know anything about guns. Do you think it would be worthwhile to teach me how to use one?"

He looks surprised. "I don't think that's a good idea with, uh..."

"I'm not sick. I'm not mental," I defend.

Justin's face becomes stern. "I don't think you're sick or mental. I just know guns and people who are emotionally compromised are not a good mix. I promise I will teach you to use one. We can go to the range one day, but until this business with Kent is settled, you aren't using any kind of weapon. Come on. We can talk inside."

He's probably right. I let it go for now, but I will learn to use that gun.

Justin works to make me a space in his room and is careful to say we don't have to sleep in the same bed if it makes me uncomfortable. He's willing to take the couch. I laugh at him. After all the things we've been doing and going through lately, that's the last thought on my mind. "You are crazy. I'll never get to sleep on my own. I need you with me, but let me have the side away from the door. You'll need visibility from that side."

"Agreed," he answers. "You're pretty good at this defense strategy. I like it." He winks as he leaves me to make another security patrol through the house. Repeatedly checking windows, doors, and the door locks.

While he's doing all of that, I decide to open a bottle of wine. We both need something to help calm our nerves. Kate and Cameron should be here tomorrow. We are going to stay with the boys until something can be done about Kate's house. Our house.

I take the bottle of wine and some glasses into Justin's bedroom and leave them on the nightstand. Then I grab my makeup bag and some pajamas and head to the bathroom. What I need right now is a hot shower and some downtime with Justin. Anything to make me forget. As I step into the bathroom, I think I should let him know what I'm doing. "Taking a shower, babe."

Justin doesn't answer. So I walk down the hall a little ways, and say, "Justin? I'm taking a shower."

I'm startled out of my skin when a voice behind me says, "Okay. I'll be here when you get out."

Releasing a sigh of relief, I turn to see Justin behind me. "Not cool, man. You scared the shit out of me!"

He laughs. "Sorry. Just needed to provide some comic relief. It's been way too tense around here tonight."

He kisses my forehead and steers me back to the bathroom. I turn on the water and then stand in front of the mirror. All I can do is stare into my own eyes. I stare so long that the image begins to blur.

Appropriate when I consider how this week has been nothing but a clusterfuck. I've done things I knew better than to do because Irma thought it was a good idea. Now look at the mess I've created. I know I'm not fully to blame, but there's no one else to explain how all of this could turn to shit so fast. I made this mess, and I'm the only one that can clean it up.

I stare at myself so long that the view gets obscured by the steam from the shower. I know that it's hot enough now. Stepping in, I lean against the wall as I let the heat sink into my skin and warm me from my toes to the top of my head.

I focus on my mantras and breathing to let go of all of the blame and guilt for what's happening all around me. I want to trust Justin and Cameron, and their police connections, to handle this whole thing. It's beyond that now.

When I've finished cleaning up and trying to let go of the day, I step into Justin's bedroom. He's kicked back on the bed. It looks like he was sitting up watching TV, waiting for me to get out, but the lack of sleep recently is evident as he is passed out cold. I pour myself a glass of wine and sit on the bed next to him. I have my cell phone in-hand so I can check on Kate.

I text Cameron, who responds that she's been sleeping a lot. We agree it's likely the Valium they're giving her to relax. She's not in a terrible amount of pain, so she's been refusing pain killers. The Valium is to help her mind calm. I start to feel sappy when I answer his last text. *"Thanks for looking out for her, Cam. You didn't have to do this."*

His answer melts my heart, *"Yes, I did. She's a great girl. No one deserves to go through anything like this. No one. I'm happy to be here with her."*

When I turn to put my phone away, Justin says something in his sleep. It startles me. I reach over and stroke the unruly hair from his forehead. With him asleep and vulnerable, I can imagine him as a little boy. As I'm basking in his sweet, restful face, he starts to speak again. This time I still and listen.

"I can take care of you. Let me help you," he pleads with someone. "I love you. Stay with me," he finishes, and my heart breaks.

11 - Confrontation

Morning arrives far too early. I finished off the bottle of wine by myself before I went to sleep. My head is making me pay for it this morning. I've called in again. I'm pretty sure I can kiss any chance of a promotion goodbye. Fact is, after this, I may need to find a new job.

Justin, on the other hand, has decided to go handle some work projects for a couple of hours. He's waiting for Cam and Kate to come home and settled. She's going to need more than a few days of rest to recover from all of the broken ribs and bruises.

All I can think about as I make us some breakfast is how I can make it up to the people I love. This hell I've unleashed on them being here has to be handled. Justin wants to help, but the only thing I can think about is resolving this myself. If I'm the one Kent wants, I'm the one he'll get. We'll put this decade of hell to an end; and soon.

We have a nice morning. I make phone calls on behalf of Kate to the homeowner's insurance to have them send a claims adjuster out. Then I call the police department for an official report number to give the claims adjuster.

Cameron brings Kate home early in the afternoon. We all get her settled into Cameron's room. She'll need an exorcism if she survives living in that room for a few days. Justin and I take turns ribbing him about his housekeeping skills (or lack thereof).

Justin dresses in his uniform, and pulls me into his room for a chat before he leaves.

"Please, for the love of God, don't do anything silly today. I'm going to be back in a couple hours. Cameron is perfectly capable of watching out for you two."

I smile and cut my eyes. "Exactly what do you mean by 'silly'?'

He's using his serious face again. "You know what I mean. You can't fix this. Stay here and let the police do their job."

"You sure think you know a lot, don't you. I'll be here with Kate. No worries. Go save the technological world and come home to me," I say calmly, betraying my true feelings. I don't want to tip him off. The less Justin knows the better.

He leans down, placing his nose to mine and staring into my eyes. "Somehow, I doubt your calm exterior. Promise me you won't get into any trouble."

I promise. And he kisses me.

℠℞℠℞℠℞℠℞℠℞℠℞

It doesn't take long for Cameron to crawl into the bed with Kate. They are drained from the whole experience. I know the kind of sleep they need. It's deep and cleansing. Something about washing the hospital off your skin, and settling into "home."

This is the moment I've been waiting for. I search through Justin's room and find the lockbox under his bed. This is where I saw him put the gun last night. I don't have any training, but I'm certain it's self-explanatory. Point it at something or someone and pull the trigger, right? It's not rocket science.

I pull the gun from the lockbox, which isn't locked. It's heavier in my hands than I thought it would be. I feel awkward trying to figure out how to hold it. Eventually, the gun rests comfortably in the palm of my right hand. I remember a friend once told me that, when I'm handling a gun, my left hand is used to steady it.

So I test this configuration of hands on the gun. *Seems legit.* I hold the gun and move around noticing how it feels to look down the top of it, pointing it at an action figure on the top of Justin's computer desk.

Satisfied I can hold it confidently, I dig for my purse, and slide it inside. I change into jeans, a T-shirt, and a ball cap borrowed from Justin's extensive collection. The irony of it being a police union hat isn't lost on me. I decide not to leave a note. I don't want any of the people I care about to come after me. They're already in too deep.

Packing the rest of my things into my rolling suitcase and makeup bag, I quietly tiptoe to the front door. I gently close the door behind me as to not wake Cam and Kate. My getaway is efficient. Right before I merge onto the interstate, my cell phone starts ringing. I feel around in my purse to find my phone and pull it out to see who's calling. It's Irma. *Oh God.*

"Hello?"

"Don't do it, baby. Stop. Turn around and go home." She demands urgently.

"What are you talking about, Mrs. Irma?" I play stupid.

She huffs before answering my question. "I've done seen it. Ya don't want to do this. This is somethin' ya can't live with. It's going ta hurt ya as much as ya want to hurt him. Please, baby, don't."

I sniffle. "I have to." My answer is just barely a whisper, and the tears are blurring my eyes. I slow the car down, and pull off into the emergency lane to finish our conversation.

"No. Ya don't have ta do anythin'. You are sinkin' to his level. Ya was born to rise. Quit lettin' him win!"

"It's the only way I'll ever be free. Then I have to think about Ethan. I haven't been a mother to him at all. He deserves better."

"Aw, baby. We can solve this together. There's hope."

"I love you Mrs. Irma. I hope this isn't the last time we talk, but I have to do this. Please understand." I disconnect the call and try to regain my resolve.

Her words are an echo in my mind. I want to do as she says, but she's never been in this situation. She's never lived as someone she's not in order to survive a man who promised to love her. She's never had to start over only to have him ruin her life again. Irma thinks she knows what's best for me, but she hasn't been hunted by Kent. I can't live in fear anymore, and I won't. There's only one way to insure that: my freedom.

I drive an hour before my cell rings again. This time I don't answer. I know who's calling. He's had plenty of time to come home and find me gone. I'm still a good ways away from the trailer Kent and I shared. I'm not even sure he lives out this far anymore, but it's a place to start looking for him.

The remainder of the drive happens on autopilot. My mind knows where I'm going, so I start to daydream the scenario of what will happen when I'm face-to-face with Kent. I imagine him sniffling and begging at the end of my gun barrel. He's a little punk who's all big and bad when he's the one in control, but turns to a weak mess when someone else takes the upper hand.

The damn cell phone never stops ringing. After Justin makes several attempts, there are calls from Cameron, Kate, and Irma. It's almost like a rotation as they each try multiple times. I don't want to turn my phone off, so I switch it to a mode that stops the ringing and vibration. This way if I need it when I confront Kent, I'll have it available.

A little over an hour later, I reach the trailer and turn onto the gravel driveway. The first thing I notice is our old mailbox is disheveled and falling over. The second thing I notice is how the trees and bushes around the driveway obscure my view of the trailer. I shake my head at how he's let the place run into the ground.

Still, as I think about the inside of that trailer and the last time I was here, panic rises in my mind. This is the home I shared with Kent and Ethan. This is where I lost my life and fought to survive so I could live. Everything looks the same, except a little more worn down.

As I pull up closer to the house, I take note of the surroundings. There's a car in the space next to the porch steps that lead up to the trailer. I'm not sure what I'll find, so as soon as I stop the car, I have my hand on the gun. Pulling the gun into my lap, and position my grip on the handle. *Ready to go.* Still, I keep looking around me to see if there are any signs he might be here. Letting Kent sneak up on me would be one of the worst ideas ever.

Speaking of worst ideas, why am I doing this? My resolve shakes. I start thinking about why I'm here and what's at stake. I have to do this.

My knees are wobbly as I force myself to get out of the car. As I close the door, I lean against the car to steady myself. For a few seconds, all I do is breathe in the fresh air around me. Cautiously, I walk up the steps. The front door is unlocked and standing open just a little bit. I try to peer in through the small opening to gauge what it is I'm walking into. All I can see is that the place has been destroyed. The smell of bad food wafts out, so bad it makes my eyes water. *Something has died in there.*

As that possibility begins to sink in, a streak of fear pierces my chest. I calm myself by thinking it could be an animal since the door is open. Using the gun to lead the way, as I saw Justin do when we went to his house the other night, I open the door and tip-toe inside.

It's quiet. The bookshelf Kent threw me into five years ago is still in a pile in the corner of the room. Part of the death smell must be the blood he never cleaned. I walk through each room more comfortably as the look of things convinces me he doesn't live here anymore. He hasn't lived here in a long time.

The toys and clothes in Ethan's room are gone. He took some pieces of furniture including the beds and random pieces like tables and a dresser. A lot of the older, more damaged things were left behind. The death smell seems strongest in the master bedroom. I slide the closet door all the way open to see I was right. It was an animal.

A raccoon is curled up in the floor of the closet and is well into the decomposition phase. I shake it off and step out on to the back porch. There's no evidence that anyone one has been out here either. Patio table and chairs are older, but intact. Some of Ethan's outside toys, like his sand box, is still here.

The adrenaline that has carried me this far is started to ebb. I'm coming down from the adrenaline high, and it settles heavily on my shoulders. I sit in a rickety old patio chair to absorb the openness of the land and woods surrounding the trailer. I'm cautious as I lay the gun in my lap and sink deeper into the chair. I focus on steadying my breathing to try and relax. Being alone out here is what I need to gain some perspective. I dwell on the things Irma said to me and how Justin begged me not do anything about Kent.

Just let the police handle it, right? They didn't handle it before. Some of that I have to own. It was my unwillingness to trust the police five years ago that allowed Kent to keep walking this planet where he ended up hurting someone I care about.

My mind circles in the same patterns that have existed since this all began. When I finally realize I have to stop putting myself in this vicious cycle where I accept all the blame for everything, the sun is setting. I think it's symbolic of the peace I've reached within myself. The sky paints the blues with oranges and tones of peach as the sun begins to lower. As the peach tones give way to the purples I adore about a southern sky, the temperatures drop and I begin to shiver. I stand to leave, and when I turn toward the door, I freeze. There he is—exactly as I remembered him.

Kent is standing on the threshold of the patio door, staring at me. He doesn't speak but rakes me in with his gaze. The cold metal of the gun forces me to remember it's still in my hand. Without a word, Kent's lips turn up at the corners, a disturbing smile, and he steps toward me. My brain says run, but my body does the opposite. I take a stand, lifting the gun so it's pointed at him. "Stop!" I cry out.

He freezes and holds his hands up innocently. "Baby! Put the gun down. There's no need for that." His voice is cool and cajoling.

"Take one more step, and I will kill you," my voice shakes as I issue the warning.

He attempts to cover his fury by molding his face into some semblance of calm. "You don't want to kill me. We're in love. Don't you remember?"

My heartbeat pounds in my ears when he says it. Like I'm some dumb child that'll fall for his charismatic salesmanship again. "What I remember, Kent, is the night you tried to kill me. Did you forget?"

"Sugarpie, I didn't try to kill you. I was drunk. It was an accident. The gun accidentally went off. I love you more than life itself. I wouldn't ever do something like that." his tone is cajoling.

"Don't 'sugarpie' me, you son of a bitch! I know what happened."

Kent is pacing side to side, not making any more advances toward me.

"Where's my son?" I ask through gritted teeth. I don't want to say my sweet boy's name to him.

He stops pacing and looks at me with the meanest glare I've ever seen. "He's our son, and you gave up your rights to him when you left me."

"Left you? Do you hear yourself? You beat me half to death our entire relationship and then you shot me. I know I ran away. I was terrified then, but I'm not anymore. Where is *my* son!" I can feel the flush on my face. I'm more afraid than I've ever been as I directly confront him. Who I used to be wouldn't have ever been so brave. I know it's pissing him off that I'm stronger than I've ever been.

"All in good time. First, we have to move you back home, and let our families know you've come back to me."

I'm stunned. He thinks I'm coming back to him or that he can scare me into coming back to him. I laugh. Emboldened, I ask, "So you move to Memphis temporarily, and then what? Stalk women until you find me?"

It's his turn to laugh, "No. I had almost given up on finding you when I moved up there. When I hired into my new sales job, I made friends with your friend Kate. She's super-hot, by the way. I was waiting at her desk for her to come back from a meeting one day and noticed the picture on her desk. It was you. You'd finally lost some weight, and you'd colored your hair, which I hate, but it was you."

"So you stalked her?"

"No, honey, I stalked you. It was hard to keep a low-profile at first. I was so excited I'd finally found you. There were several times when I could have grabbed you and disappeared. But what's the fun in that? Then I saw how close you two were and decided that the best way to get to you would be through her. By the way, how is she? Did they tape up all the broken ribs? Put salve on all the bruises?" His smile is sadistic.

Rage is filtering through my body when I answer, "She's fine. Don't you worry about Kate. You'll never have the chance to hurt anyone else. Especially her."

His smile fades. "What about your little lover boy? What's his name? Justin? Can I hurt him?"

"Leave him out of this."

"Now, how can I do that? He's had his hands all over you." There's a shift in his features. He looks scary when he proclaims, "You are my wife! I'll kill him for touching you."

There has to be a smarter way to do this. I decide to taunt him since this seems to upset him. "He's twice the lover you ever were, Kent. He's tender, slow, and can make me..."

I don't finish because he lunges at me. When he does, my reaction is to squeeze the trigger of the gun. The blast is loud; so much louder than I ever imagined it would be. Louder than I remember when Kent shot me.

It makes my ears ring and my whole arm aches with the recoil from the gun. I try to hold on to it, but the vibration causes me to drop it. *Shit! This is why you need training.*

The shot slowed him down, but I missed. The fury in his features as he lands a backhanded slap across my face. There's a faint taste of blood in my mouth, and all I can think is he's only gotten better at this over the years. I double over and hold my face, wiping at the blood in the corner of my mouth.

When I do, Kent grabs me by my hair and pulls me back into the trailer, where he slings me to the floor. There's a searing pain up my right arm when I land in the pile of trash. I bite the inside of my cheek and groan to keep from crying. I don't want to give him the satisfaction of knowing he really hurt me.

I'm on all fours, trying to get to my feet, when he kicks me in my left ribs. The wind is knocked out of my body and I collapse on the floor.

"Fucking whore."

12 - Recompense

Kent goes back out to the patio for the gun. I lay frozen on the floor, terrified to move. I'm waiting for him to come back and finish the job he started once before when lights fill the trailer. I can barely hear the purr of engines when Kent walks back through. He's talking under his breath, then looks at me and says, "If you don't want anyone else hurt, keep your stupid mouth shut." He tucks the gun in the waistband of his pants, right at his lower back.

The voice I hear when Kent answers the door is Justin's. Hope renews inside me, and I try to get back on my feet. When I fall over, Justin must hear the thump because then there's a commotion at the door. I finally use the back of the couch to pull myself up onto my feet. My arm feels broken, and I hold it across my body.

As I'm standing there, Justin and Kent rolling on the floor, fighting for control of the gun. When I'm about to jump in and help Justin, another man rushes through the front door.

"Police! Freeze! Stop now, or I'll shoot the both of you!"

He's an older man, dressed in a police uniform. He's got his own gun drawn on the guys. They stop fighting and sit up gasping for breath, glaring at each other. The police officer looks around the room when they surrender. His eyes land on me. "Ma'am, are you Alana Thomas?"

I swallow before answering. "Yes, sir."

"Are you hurt?"

"Yes sir."

"Stay there for now. Let me get these two hooked." He reaches for the little speaker thing on his shoulder and says some code stuff I don't understand. Then he points the gun at Justin, "If you move, I will shoot you."

Justin puts his hands up and slides away from Kent. "Okay, Paul. Just do what you gotta do."

Paul? Who is Paul?

The officer, Paul, puts Kent in handcuffs. When he stands Kent up and marches him out the front door, Kent winks at me then blows me a kiss. I close my eyes and look away. I open them when I feel someone approach me. It's Justin.

"Hey. You okay?" his voice is gentle, his eyes searching.

"No."

"I knew the answer to that, but I had to ask. Do you think you need an ambulance?"

I shake my head. "No. You can drive me to the hospital."

He smiles. "Okay. I can do that. We'll have to do a report before we can go. So, uh, doesn't look like he lives here anymore."

"It doesn't. See the smashed bookcase?"

He looks around the room and then back at me.

"Me. That happened the night he shot me."

He turns back to me, concern etched across his face. "Do you need to get out of here? You can sit in the car while Paul takes your statement."

I take a moment to think before I answer. "I'm actually pretty good right now. I was trying to find out from Kent where he's stashed Ethan. He wouldn't tell me."

Justin is checking out my arm, tenderly prodding, when he absently says, "We have Ethan. I found him. He's at the station with Department of Human Services."

"What!"

This time he looks up at me. "What did you think I went to take care of today? I knew with Kent pulling this psycho bullshit, Ethan didn't need to be anywhere around him. I called Paul and we've been doing the leg-work to lay hands on him."

My heart swells. I can't form a coherent thought. Elation being my primary emotion, immediately followed with fear. *What if he doesn't want me?* The thought is sobering. He may not want to see me after I left him like I did. Or did he believe I was dead? What did Kent tell him? I'm brought back to reality when Justin dabs at the blood on my face a bit. "Ouch! That stings!"

"Sorry. I was just checking out how badly you're hurt. Looks like your arm is broken. Maybe a couple ribs, too." He can't seem to stop touching me as he's speaking. It's like he's physically restrained from crushing me against him.

"Yeah, that's what I was thinking. Will you hold me?"

Justin's gaze meets mine. "Thought you'd never ask. I didn't want to hurt you." As the words leave his lips, he gently folds himself around me. I hadn't realized I was shaking until that moment. As his sturdy body provides mine with warmth and stability, something inside me breaks. I start sobbing from deep within me. Kent is in handcuffs, Ethan is safe, and I have Justin here with me. Still, it doesn't feel like this nightmare is over yet.

Justin starts to make soothing noises into my hair as he holds me. This is my favorite part of him holding me. He can calm my nerves in nearly an instant. It's a strange time to say it, but it needs to be said. I pull back a tiny bit and look up to find his eyes. I need him to feel me when I say it, "I want strings."

"We are so far past strings. You got strings and anything else you want with them. I love you." He smiles at me lovingly.

"I would be dead if you hadn't been persistent in finding him," I tell him soberly.

He nods slowly. "I know. By the way, how did my gun get here?"

I shrug. "It seemed fairly easy to use a gun. I, uh, was going to..."

He puts his hand over my mouth. "Don't say it out loud. I know what you thought you were doing. Do you agree that it was not your smartest decision?"

I sigh. "Yes, Dad. I agree. But do you agree that you need to equip me properly in the future?"

He frowns. "Yes. I can see now that you need to be trained. A wild card like you needs skills."

Paul clears his throat. "Excuse me Ms. Thomas. I have some questions to ask you."

୫୦୯୫୨୦୯୫୨୦୯୫୨୦୯୫୨୦୯୫

Justin and I spent about an hour answering questions. I explained to Paul that Kent is, legally, my husband. We also discussed the incident five years ago when he nearly killed me and how I fled for my life. I gave him the name of the officer outside of Memphis who helped me change my name to validate my story. Then the biggest question came up, "What are you doing here tonight? Mr. Walsh said the gun is yours. Can you please explain?"

Against Justin's advice, and my own better judgment, I explained. I went into great detail about how he has terrorized Kate, the kidnapping, the physical assault, and the threat against my own life. I acted under great duress when I drove to the trailer to find Kent and confront him. Justin can't look at me while I explain. I know why. He's afraid I'll be charged with something. In the end, I tell Paul I didn't intend to kill Kent. I wanted to scare him away, and get information about Ethan. I brought the gun as protection in case he tried to attack me again.

Paul takes a lot of notes and tells me Kent is being charged with assault with a deadly weapon, and we'll have our day in court. Unofficially, he tells me to get an attorney. Kent could easily turn this back on me since I could be viewed as the aggressor.

As I am no longer involved with Kent, my showing up on a property he owns with a gun could be misconstrued. The thought sickens me. I should have listened to Justin when he told me to let the police handle it. I had no idea my actions could backfire and put me in the hot seat. For the second time, Kent nearly killed me, and I may be at fault for it.

When we finish with Paul and our statements, Justin drives me to the hospital. The symmetry of the moment shakes me to the core. This moment is all too familiar. He drove me to the hospital the last time Kent attacked me. I reach my left hand across the console to grab his hand lying on his leg. "Hey, I'm not as bad off as the last time you had to drive me after a Kent attack."

He doesn't smile. "I know."

"You're still pissed."

He sighs, "I'm not pissed. I can't comprehend why you would do this. Why would you put yourself in this situation again? I told you we could handle it."

I don't answer. His questions hang in the air between us.

ॐ♋ॐ♋ॐ♋ॐ♋ॐ♋ॐ♋

After several hours of testing, x-rays, and some pain medication, my list of injuries include: a broken right arm, two cracked ribs, some bruises, and a really hard head. Nothing to do but cast my arm and tape my ribs. The rest will heal on their own. The ride home is too quiet. Justin's silence concerns me.

"When can I see Ethan?"

He shrugs. "When DHS finishes with him, I guess."

"What do you mean, 'finishes with him?' Is there something wrong with him?"

He shakes his head. "No. We found him in the apartment Kent leased in Memphis. He's a little malnourished, and he's never been to school. Kent didn't let him out much, so he's not been very verbal with us. They just want to check him over."

My heart sinks like an anchor. My buoyant feeling at knowing he is safe becomes a shattered emotion. "But he's okay?" I ask again.

Justin nods. "He'll be fine. I'm sure of it. He's going to have a hard road ahead of him."

"He was in Memphis? All this time?"

"Yeah, he was less than three miles from you."

"I can't believe that. How strange that is! Well, not strange. Kent told me he was stalking me. He knew about you. He—" I swallow. "—made threats against you. I should have killed him. Anyway, let's forget about Kent. I can't wait to see Ethan so I can squeeze him and kiss his sweet face."

"Alana," he pauses. "DHS may not let you have him until the case with Kent is cleared. If you pick up a charge, they'll have to find another family member to take Ethan."

"No! They can't do that. He's mine." Tears start to prick my eyes.

"Honey, they can, and they will. Actions have consequences. You acted in a way you thought you had to, so maybe that will help your case, but you need to come to terms with what may happen as a result."

Heartbreak floods my whole body. Justin is holding my hand as we drive. The idea that Kent could still keep me from my boy is beyond comprehension. "What about temporary insanity?"

"We have to prove it, but I think we can. There's evidence in Kent's apartment that he was stalking you. Paul had a team go in to document the place and collect all the evidence. I'm going to call a friend of mine who's an attorney to help us with your case."

"What kind of evidence was in the apartment?"

His answer is almost curt. "You don't want to know right now. I'll give you a list once they're done processing it." Protection mode is intact, I see.

"All right. You're right, I may have had my fill of Kent and creepiness. By the way, who is Paul?"

He gives me a half-smile. "My old sergeant. I called him to help me with you and this whole situation. He was actually kind of shocked I'd found you, let alone fallen for you."

My eyes widen. "Fallen for me?"

"Completely."

13 - Dawn

I've always thought the most beautiful part of the day was sunset. Today has changed my mind. I'll always see sunset as an amazingly beautiful feature of nature, but dawn has become my new favorite. Something about the new day bringing a renewed hope for all of life. I'm full of gratitude when I see the dawn as an opportunity to start over. And we get a do-over every single day.

It's been a week since Kent was arrested. Kate and I are still staying with the boys. She's gone through the process of getting the insurance claims filed to fix the house. Somehow, though, we just don't feel safe going home. Cameron and Kate have been spending an inordinate amount of time together in his room. He hardly goes to work, and she's out of a job.

She quit as soon as she recovered from the attack. There's a nagging in the back of my mind that says she should be able to file suit against the company she was working for. She followed the process and told them about the harassment from Kent. They said they were investigating, but did nothing. I'm sure if she did file a suit, they would cover by producing paperwork that shows they were working it.

It doesn't matter. Kate doesn't want anything else to do with that company. She's been looking for work, but the job market has slim pickings. I'm sure something will pan out for her.

Justin is taking me to meet his friend who is a lawyer. He's going to help me with my case. Justin is certain that there won't be any charges filed against me. The history between Kent and I should help me get some kind of temporary insanity if it comes down to it. I don't know how all that works, but it seems logical. It's overwhelming to think Kent could still affect my life after all that's happened.

I have been uncharacteristically clingy with Justin, too. I can't sit still in the house unless he's right there with me. Often times, I'm waking up with nightmares. New nightmares. Ones where Kent hurts or kills Justin. All they do is make me more dependent on Justin, and I cling to him to know he's okay. That we're okay. I hate that I can't seem to stand on my own two feet.

Sometimes the weight of everything that's happened in the last month is enough to make me weak in the knees. Justin is a good place to lean when that happens. He's been everything I've needed every day. Almost like a freaking movie. I could have never imagined finding someone so great.

The impact of this realization brings to mind that I haven't told Justin how thankful I am for him. When we pull into the parking lot of Mr. Rosa's office, and I turn to Justin. "Hey, before we go in, I need to tell you something."

He looks surprised, but he reaches over taking my hand and looks into my eyes earnestly. "Okay?"

I take a deep breath. "Thank you. I wouldn't be able to get through any of this without you. Most of the time, I'm still a mess in my own head, but I know I can rely on you to steady me and keep me moving forward. I don't think I've said it enough. I don't think I'll ever be able to say it enough."

Justin smiles. "I told you, you have so much more than strings. We're in everything together. Always."

Emotions well up inside me, and I sniffle. "Always." I want to tell him I love him, too. He managed to say it, but I haven't said it back yet. *Now isn't the time. He'll think I'm saying it because I'm scared.*

ℬ☯ℭℬ☯ℭℬ☯ℭℬ☯ℭℬ

Mr. Rosa is a stout Hispanic man with a genial smile. His cheeks are so round they close off his eyes when he smiles. I immediately love him. He greets us both with back-cracking hugs, then ushers us into his office.

His administrative assistant brings us coffee and a tray of pastries. It's all I can do not to shove an entire apple fritter into my mouth. I'm a stress eater, and I can admit that. I own it. However, knowing what's at stake, I can't do it. Though, I consider taking one for the road when we're done.

"So, Ms. Thomas," Mr. Rosa begins. "You have some trouble we need to take care of. Care to tell me what happened? In your own words, of course. I've read the police report, but those can be skewed to the favor of the police. No offense, Mr. Ellis."

Justin scoffs. "Mr. Ellis? Seriously, Manuel? After all these years?

Mr. Rosa chuckles. "Okay. Right, Justin. Your story, Ms. Thomas."

"Well, sir, Kent is my husband. Soon to be ex-husband if you can help me with that, too. You see, five years ago he tried to kill me. I survived because of the kindness of strangers, and I was able to start over. Over the last month or so, my roommate, Kate, has told me about a man at work who was sexually harassing her. I didn't know it was Kent.

"Roughly a week ago, she was kidnapped and attacked. When I saw her in the hospital, Kate told me who had done it. I lost it. I was terrified because I believed he had found me, and had attacked Kate because of me. So when Justin went to work one day, I got his gun from the lockbox under his bed." I can't help myself, I look up at Justin when I tell this part. "I'm sorry," I say.

He smiles at me lovingly and mouths the words, "It's okay." Then he squeezes my hand. I hadn't even realized he was holding it.

A tear rolls down my cheek, and I quickly wipe it away before continuing. "I drove to the trailer we lived in together. I didn't know if he'd be there, but I was convinced if I left it up to the police he would get away with it. You see, he's very charismatic. People fall under some kind of spell around him. He had abused me for years, and no matter how many people I reached out to for help, they didn't believe me. Not even my own family. So, I needed to confront him to put all of this conflict to an end."

At this Mr. Rosa interjects, "Did you intend to harm Mr. Walsh?"

I think for a moment. "Is this discussion just between us?"

Mr. Rosa tells me that anything we discuss is covered by privilege, and he can't tell anyone unless we agree he can.

I straighten my back, and tell the truth. "No. My plan was simple: kill Kent and take custody of our boy. I told the police that I just wanted to confront him, and the gun was for protection."

Shock crosses his face. "Okay, maybe we leave out the murder plot when we meet with the district attorney and DHS."

I nod. "Whatever you think is best, sir. Remember, I've been living a false life, without my son, for five years. Kent stole everything from me. He shot me. Willpower carried me away from that trailer with nothing. So when he showed up again and attacked my roommate after stalking me, I had to do something."

He lets out a hearty laugh. "You're probably right, but like I said, you leave the taking to me. Tell me how this has affected your life today."

"I have no life. I've taken a leave of absence from work, and my roommate has lost her job. Well, she quit. Our home is under repair, so we're living with Justin and his roommate for now.

Mr. Rosa tells us about his strategy. I'm thankful Justin is here, again, because I really don't understand everything he tells us. I feel slightly guilty that in all of the time we've been in his office, neither Justin or I touch the pastries.

As we're shaking hands, and saying our goodbyes, I make my apologies. "Mr. Rosa, please thank your admin for the pastries. I'm sorry we didn't eat any."

"Oh, honey, don't you worry. My wife will understand. Whatever we don't eat here, we take to our kids or to the homeless shelter."

"I didn't realize that was Mrs. Rosa."

"Yes. She's been helping me in the office until I can find an admin. It's been pretty tough to find someone reliable with experience in a legal office."

"I know someone who is a great admin, completely reliable, and has experience in a legal office. She's new to the job search. Although, I don't want it to be considered a conflict of interest."

His face is serious when he says, "Please give me her name and contact information. I'll work out conflict of interest nonsense."

When we leave Mr. Rosa's office, Justin takes me to an amazing lunch spot. It's a hole in the wall Mexican place. He's greeted by the host, and they talk for a while in Spanish.

I'm floored because I had no idea Justin spoke another language. Shows we still have a ton to learn about each other. He introduces me, and we are seated in a secluded booth at the back of the restaurant.

"Woah, Mr. World here. Do you know someone everywhere we go?"

He laughs. "Not everywhere, I make friends fast."

I give him a look of disbelief. "And where did you learn Spanish?"

His look is dubious. "I pick up a little here and a little there."

"Are you seriously holding out on me?"

"Nah. I don't have a straight answer for how I know stuff like that."

I decide to let it go; it's not important right now. I change the subject, "Do you have plans for the rest of the day?"

Justin thinks for a moment, then shakes his head. "Nope. Just me and you today."

His devilish smile is enchanting. I consider our options, then remember Kate and Cameron are at the house. I mentally groan.

He interrupts my thoughts, "What'd you have in mind?'

"Oh, I was thinking I would like to take you to meet someone. Someone who's important to me."

"I would love to meet anyone you think is important. Who is it?'

"Let's finish eating, and I'll drive."

"This is very mysterious. I like it!"

When we pull up to Irma's house, I see a familiar truck parked in the driveway. I'm almost bouncing in my seat. Justin notices.

"Getting more than you bargained for here? Is it a good thing?" he asks.

"Oh. My. God. It is such a good thing. It's Rhae and Cade! God, I hope it's both of them anyway." I slam the car in park and jump out, running for the porch. By the time I'm on the first step, Rhae is running down them toward me. We collide in a tackle-hug and fall backward onto the yard.

"Oh, my God! Could you have called to tell me you were coming up?" I yell through tears into her hair as I'm squeezing her for dear life.

She's just as breathless as she tries to answer me, "Where's the fun in calling ahead? We decided last night to make the drive. We arrived early this morning! So are you going to introduce me to the hottie?"

"Shit! Yes. Of course. How silly of me! I just got so excited to see you. And Cade is here, too?"

"Cade's here. He's inside with Irma. She's...well, she's not doing so good."

In all the hell I've been dealing with, I let Irma slip my focus. "God, Rhae, I'm so sorry. When did you find out?"

"She finally told Cade last week."

"Okay, we'll get inside with her in a minute let me introduce you to Justin. Do not call him a hottie. Please?"

"Whatever."

We climb the porch steps where Justin and Cade have taken up residence on the porch swing. They are chatting about guy things. I have no idea what. Mentally, I imagine it's something like guns, trucks, huntin' and whatnot. It's a stereotypical way to think of them, and I try to stop. *Nope, can't.*

"Rhae." I gesture to her. "This is Justin." I finish with a gesture to Justin.

Rhae extends her hand, all business. "Nice to meet you, Justin."

"I assume you boys have met?" I say, continuing with introductions.

Cade speaks up, "Yep. We're good. Let's go inside."

Irma isn't stirring around her kitchen. It's odd and a little unsettling. I turn to Cade. "Where is she?"

Cade stares at his shoes, uncomfortable. "She's in her room. Likely lying down."

"What's going on?" I ask, upset now.

Rhae wraps her arm around my shoulder. "Let's go sit down and talk."

Cade and Rhae proceed to tell me Irma has cancer. It's an inoperable brain tumor. She's been feeling bad for a while but didn't want to say anything to anyone. She didn't want us all upset or rushing to her side instead of living our lives. She's on medication that should keep her comfortable until the end. Which, the doctors say, will be soon.

My heart cracks wide open. Numbness floods through my limbs as I sit dazed, listening to all the information they lay out for me. My gut-instinct is action. "So that's it? We just take their word for it? There's nothing that we can do?"

Justin reaches out to comfort me, and I pull away. I stand, staring at all of them. "How can you be okay with this? This isn't acceptable. We have to find some research study. We have to look into holistic care. Something out there will help her."

Rhae stands and meets me toe-to-toe. "What kind of life would it be for her? You know her. She wants a quality of life. She doesn't want to run back and forth to Memphis for treatments that will make her sicker than they will help to cure the cancer. Anything we try will go against her wishes."

Defeated, knowing Rhae is right, I flop down into a chair. I sit and process everything they've said. I know there's nothing to be done. Irma has always been a force to be reckoned with, at least during the time I've known her. After several minutes, I stand. "Okay well, I came here to introduce her to Justin. Let's go."

We walk quietly down the hall, not knowing if she's asleep or not. When I crack the door open, she looks like she could be asleep, but then she turns her head and sees me.

"Oh baby! Get in here. Bring that boy a yers in here too."

I can't help the beaming smile I give her as we step into the room. "Hello, my love," I whisper as I bend down to hug her neck.

She whispers back, so that only I can hear her, "I see you found him."

I pull back, surprised. "It's him? The one you knew I would find."

Her sweet face is bright with life and light when she says. "It is."

I stand up fully and tug Justin toward her bed. "Justin, this is the incomparable Mrs. Irma."

14 - Beginnings

I've had several meetings with DHS regarding Ethan. The lady assigned to work with me, Dinah, is very kind. She seems to be sympathetic to my situation. Although, she never gives anything away about what her decision will be. She's very clear that until I can resolve the case that's pending, there will be no decision about what can happen about Ethan. It's been very painful for me, but she's made me identify some family members who can either vouch for my character or would be willing to take Ethan.

I named my mother and my aunt Sissy. Sissy used to spend a ton of time with me because she thought my mother was insane. In some ways, I think my mother always blamed Sissy for my wild streak. Sissy is a buxom red-haired, six-foot-tall ball of fire. She disagreed with the strict upbringing my parents gave me. She thought they should have allowed me to explore and experiment. In my own parenting, I think I used a happy mix of both styles. Ethan was only three the last time I saw him. Not much exploring and experimenting a child that age can do.

Depending on what Dinah wants to know about me, she'll get what she wants from one or the other. Although, their representations of my character could conflict. I pray not.

Dinah has agreed to let me see Ethan under supervision. Today is the day! I'm up and dressed much earlier than I need to be. My legs won't stop bouncing as I sit on the edge of the couch and watch the clock.

Justin staggers into the living room, hungover from sleep. "Anxious?"

"I'm so much more than anxious. Seeing him is everything. I don't know if he'll remember me. If he does remember me, does he still want me to be his mother? Has he given up on me? What do I do if he doesn't want me anymore?"

He takes a seat beside me and places his hand on my bouncing leg. "Stop. You're making yourself crazy for nothing. He's going to love you. You're his mother. That's a bond no one can break. No matter what. Hang on to that."

"What if he thinks I'm stupid or lame or whatever?"

"Just be you. He'll love you for who you are. Plus, aren't all parents supposed to be lame and stupid?"

I laugh. "I know. I'm so nervous."

"Do you want me to go with you?"

I shake my head. "No. Thanks, though. I have to do this on my own. I have to reconnect with him on my own first. I just wish I knew how this will work out. I need Kent convicted and sentenced. I need my case resolved. I need to know Ethan wants me. All the stars have to align for me to have him back."

"The stars are aligning. All of this will be fine."

I grab his hand and squeeze. "I know. Are you sure you're okay that I have a son? That our lives are going to change if I get him?"

His smile is proud. "Not if. When. He'll be yours again, and I'm totally okay with it. I'll admit it kind of freaks me out, but in a good way.

"I'm not even sure how you can be freaked out in a good way."

"I mean that this is a little person I can spend guy time with him. You know teaching him baseball and all that manly stuff. I mean, when you look at it the right way, it's awesome. Are you sure you're okay with me filling that kind of role for him?"

I'm surprised by this question because it's not something I've considered. I think for a moment. "Yeah. I'm good with it." We sit in silence a little longer. "I'm really good with it," I stare into Justin's eyes when I say it. "One more thing. I wanted to say this when the stress was off so you would know how much I really mean it."

"What is it," he asks.

"I love you."

His face fills with light right before he leans down and kisses me. He wraps me up in his warm, strong arms, and it feels like he's trying to infuse me with his strength and confidence. "I sincerely wish you would let me go with you. I don't like you being out in the world alone," he whispers against the top of my head as he kisses me there tenderly.

I sigh. "I know. But you can't be with me at all times. I can do this. I'll stay out of trouble. Promise."

୧୬ଓ୨୧ଓ୨୧ଓ୨୧ଓ୨

I arrive fifteen minutes early for my time with Ethan. Dinah meets me at the entrance, and takes me into her office.

"There have been some developments in the unresolved business," Dinah starts.

"Okay."

She smiles. "I'll give you the good news first. There was enough evidence against Kent from your statement and Kate's account of her attack that he's been, basically, forced into a guilty plea. The judge is sentencing him tomorrow. I spoke with your attorney, he said you were welcome to attend, but you don't have to if you think it would be too much."

The air is forced out of my lungs. It's everything I've been praying would happen in Kent's case. "How many years is he looking at?" I ask timidly.

"I don't know, but it seems like it's going to be a lot. Now, for the bad news."

I brace myself. "Give it to me."

She takes a deep breath. "Ethan's foster parents have been concerned. He's been somewhat violent with other children in the home. They asked that we have him evaluated by a psychologist. What we found out from of these sessions is disturbing. Are you ready for this?"

I nod hesitantly as I knot my hands in my lap.

"Kent was emotionally abusive to him. He threatened him with disownment or that he would give him away. Ethan has been effectively non-verbal except in session with the doctor. The only thing he's told the doctor is you were dead. His dad told him that. When he meets you, it's going to be a shock for him. The doctor has been laying the ground work for us to re-introduce you to him, but, I warn you, it may be rough."

Processing what she's telling me is shattering. Kent didn't lay a hand on him, but emotionally abused him. He berated him. A small, eight-year-old little boy. Of course he did. My emotions range from rage to guilt.

"I did this," I mutter as I wipe away tears.

Dinah looks puzzled. "Ma'am?"

I shake my head. "I'm to blame. I left him there. I knew what a monster Kent was, and I left him there to save my own ass."

She walks around her desk to take the seat next to me. "Alana, if you are going to fix any of this, you're going to need to talk to someone. A psychologist. You're just as damaged as Ethan, if not more so. You can't expect this to be a quick reunion and that everything Kent did to both of you will magically disappear."

I swallow as guilt floods through me. "I know. I'll do whatever it takes to get him back."

She smiles. "I knew that would be your answer. Your Aunt Sissy, knew it too. She told me no one deserved to have Ethan back more than you."

"I have to ask, did you call my mother?"

She nods. "It didn't go well. She said her daughter died five years ago and hung up on me."

I'm not surprised at all. "Can we see Ethan now?"

ᏇᏇᏇᏇᏇᏇᏇᏇᏇ

Dinah leads me to a large room furnished like a comfortable living room, only there's no TV. She explains that TV detracts from the necessary parental interactions. She leaves me alone while she goes to get Ethan. I walk over by the window and try to put my strong mask in place. The last thing he needs is to see his mother for the first time and she's a mess.

I hear the door behind me open and close. When I turn around, I see him. He's taller, and his baby face is turning into a more firm, masculine version of my face. He stops barely inside the doorway, and turns to look at Dinah. He seems to be confused. Then after a few looks between Dinah and I he says, "That's my mom!"

My heart melts, and I can't help crying all over again. I want him to take this at his own pace and not rush him. So I stand by the windows and study his bronzed brown hair and those green eyes. They are piercing. He's slightly skinnier than I thought he'd be, but there's absolutely no doubt he's mine. The craving in my chest to hug him becomes too much, and I take a step toward him.

"Hello, Ethan. Can I hug you?" I ask.

He nods and runs toward me.

I drop to my knees and absorb the impact of him hitting me full-force. All I can do is hold him and breathe in his scent. He has always had this slight Play-Doh smell about him, and he still has it. As I'm absorbing every possible detail of him, I feel him start to shudder. Then he takes in a breath, and I know he's crying.

I pull back to look at him, and he says, "You were dead. Daddy said you died. How are you here?"

"Oh, baby, we have many things to talk about. All you need to know is I'm real, and I love you. We'll be together all the time soon."

He turns to look at Dinah. "Do I have to go back to foster care? Can't I go home with my mom now?"

Dinah and I sit him down to explain that there a few things we have to take care of, but he can see me as often as he would like until that's all take care of. He's not happy, and when our visitation time is up, he cries. He doesn't want me to leave him. His heartbreak echoes my own. I ask him to be patient and be nice to the other kids at foster care. He promises me and reluctantly leaves with Dinah.

When he's out of sight, I leave. The first thing I do in the car is call Mr. Rosa to ask about my case.

"Alana, my darling," he says. "We have a meeting with the district attorney tomorrow. I was about to call you."

I sigh, relieved. "Thank you. Have you hired an admin yet? You know, we can't have a high-powered attorney like yourself making phone calls on your own."

He chuckles. "You are behind. Lots of news happening today. I met Kate, and she's going to start for me next week!"

"Fantastic! Give me all the details on this meeting."

He tells me where to be, reminds me he'll do all the talking, and then we hang up.

ᔕᘍᑫᔕᘍᑫᔕᘍᑫᔕᘍᑫᔕᘍᑫ

I pull up to Justin's place as Kate and Cameron are loading Kate's car with her suitcases.

"Hey, what's up?" I ask, getting out of the car.

Kate hugs me. "The contractor called. We can move back in the house. Come on, I'll help you pack up."

I hesitate as I feel like a weight has been dropped in my stomach. "Kate," I start. "I can't leave here. Not yet."

"What's wrong? Of course you can, you need to come home with me."

I shake my head. "I think, for now, I want to stay right here with Justin. And then..." I swallow. I hadn't thought about this until this moment.

When Ethan comes home, we'll need our own place. I have to provide a life for him. Not that living with Kate would be a bad thing. We need a place that's ours. This is a fresh start, a new beginning, for both of us. We need a life untouched by pain, hurt, death, and Kent. "Kate, I'm getting my son back. We're going to have to find a place that's just for us."

Kate nods. She doesn't make me explain. She knows why I need to do this. I help her finish load the car, and she squeezes me extra hard right before she leaves. My heart swells because she will always be a sister to me.

15 - Happy

"Watch out!" I shout as I hear a box *thud* against the floor. I stick my head around the corner to see Cameron, red-faced, leaning against the wall, huffing. He's just lugged a box of my books up the stairs and dropped them in front of the apartment door. "Oh, sorry, Cam. Don't bust my books up dropping the boxes like that."

He glares.

Justin glides lithely up the stairs with a box of linens and neatly shoves Cam with his shoulder when he passes. "You okay, buddy? Do we need to start working out again? Eating Kate's food and being her slave day and night is not agreeing with your physical needs, man."

Cameron doesn't laugh, only sulks down the steps to retrieve more boxes.

Moving day hasn't been a happy experience for me in a very long time. Today is different. Today marks the start of my happily ever after. Cameron and Justin are helping me settle in before I collect Ethan from foster care and bring him home for good.

We've had some amazing supervised visits. In the last month, they've been less supervised as Dinah made her decision that I could have him. Ethan's done well with counseling. He wanted me to attend the sessions with him, and the psychologist thought that was a great idea. Together we've been working toward building a life that is healthy and happy.

I'm aware, more than Ethan is, that life won't always be an episode of *Leave it to Beaver*. Those cheesy happy faces you see on TV are a façade, and I know it. But we have an opportunity to be together, and to try to overcome the darkness and demons that haunt our dreams. The dreams and nightmares are shifting. There's less fear and more hope. For that, I'm thankful.

Justin was disappointed when I told him that I didn't want to live with him. He understands Ethan and I need this. We need to be a family first, and anyone else will have to work themselves in over time.

Building a bond and a trust with Ethan is my top priority. Further, Ethan needs to get settled into school. In an effort to control him, Kent had been "homeschooling.".

This kept him from making friends outside of his dad, which partially explains his reluctance to be open with the psychologist at first. Plus, his lack of interaction with other kids explains his infrequent violent outbursts in foster care.

At eight years old, he didn't know how to work and play with other children. All of which has gotten better with the right attention and guidance.

Recently, Dinah and I took him to the school he'll attend and had his competency in core subjects tested. He scored off the charts with reading, but barely third grade level for all other subjects. Still it was enough to enroll him with his proper age group. We also met with the counselor for his grade, and the teachers she recommended he be with for his first year of public school. They have all expressed commitments to watching out for him and understanding his background. His needs are different from that of other children his age. Together, I think we'll be able to have a successful year. Initially, Ethan was scared of the school, and we worked through that together. He seems to be looking forward to recess the most!

೫೦൦ﬡ೫೦൦ﬡ೫೦ﬡ೫೦ൠﬡ೫೦ﬡ

"Deep thoughts?" Justin whispers softly in my ear as he wraps his arms around my waist from behind.

I'm startled because I hadn't realized I was frozen in my unpacking of the wineglasses. Lost in my own thoughts, Justin had the chance to sneak up on me. My answer is nothing more than a sound effect, "Mmhmm."

He hums in my ear before saying, "Cameron and Kate went home. We have everything unloaded."

Leaning back in his arms, I nuzzle under his chin, and drop a small kiss there. "So we're alone?"

"We are," he growls in a low voice. "Do you know how long it's been since we've been alone?" He plants kisses slowly from the top of my head, then behind my ear, and starts down my neck.

Shivers run down my spine, and my skin turns into goosebumps. "I quit counting. I'm sorry it's been so long." My words are barely a mutter.

Still trailing kisses across the back of my neck and onto my shoulders, he whispers, "*Shhhhh*. Let me seduce you."

I laugh. "I prefer to be wooed."

Frustrated now, he says, "If you would stop talking, I would woo you."

Turning, I lift my arms and wrap them around the back of his neck and whisper, "Woo me, baby," before I kiss the tip of his nose then offer my mouth to him.

೮෯ഔ෯ഔ෯ഔ෯ഔ෯ഔ෯ଔ

We make love in my disheveled apartment all afternoon and fall asleep wrapped around each other in the middle of the living room floor. I'm startled awake by my cell phone. When I sit up, I'm disoriented. It feels like I've been asleep for a hundred years and have no concept of what a cell phone is. "Fuck!" I say to no one when I jump up and run to grab it, but whoever it was hung up. I quickly unlock it to see I've missed a call from Rhae. Immediately, I call back.

"Hey! I'm sorry I couldn't get to the phone fast enough."

Her answer is a sniffle. "Irma passed."

My breath catches in my throat, and my mind begins to spin. "What?"

"We knew she didn't have long. It happened this morning. She just didn't wake up."

Tears are flowing down my cheeks, and I try to staunch the sound in my voice when I ask, "What do you need me to do?"

Her answer is calm, "Nothing. Irma took care of her own arrangements. All we have to do is show up."

I smile. "That was her way. We'll be there. Tell me when and where."

Two days later, Justin, Ethan and I are at Irma's funeral. It's a dichotomy of emotion as we are sad to have lost her, but her instructions were for her funeral to be a celebration. There are balloons and streamers everywhere.

The flowers are beautiful lilies selected by Irma to make it bright and cheerful. She always told me roses were for lovers and not for funerals. Rhae and Cade look exhausted, but are all smiles through their tears. The music is bright and ever-so-Irma. Her end is as big as her life was.

The preacher she asked to speak seems to be a bit drunk. My suspicions are confirmed when he slurs his words. I don't hear most of his sermon, but my ears perk up when he talks about how she helped him. How he was lost and wandering alone until he crossed paths with a woman of immense strength and vision.

Then he instructs us via letter from Irma, "Go forth and celebrate life. My life isn't ending, it's beginning. I've been waiting for the day when I would be with my husband again and feel his love once more. I've waited for the day I would meet my savior and have every question I've ever wondered answered.

"Don't think for one minute I've given up watching over my babies. You are all my babies by blood and by heart. Rhae, I'm going to meet your mama. We have things to discuss, and I have a full update for her. Cade, you are the best of us. Take care of your sweet Rhae. Make her your bride already! Alana, my sweet girl. You have so much life ahead of you. There are so many things coming your way, and you will be great at handling all of them. Love that boy of yours."

My heart breaks with joy and fear at the words in her letter. I know there are so many more obstacles coming. But that's life. A life I have to live. A life that is full of hope and possibility! *How cheesy*. I've never felt optimistic before, and it rather skeeves me out.

I escaped all charges in the incident with Kent and returned to work as if nothing ever happened. All around me are miracles. None of this should have happened the way that it did, yet it's perfect that it happened.

The thing about getting through tough situations is that when you look back, you can see how things that seemed to be all wrong and a mess were really in the plan and had to happen so much better times would come.

If there's one thing I've learned in this crazy life I've lived, it's that you have to embrace the bad to get to the good. And the good is pretty great.

About the Author

Meg Farrell was born and raised in Mississippi where she and her husband, Jason, still make their home. The Farrells have 3 children, 3 surly cats, and 2 sweet dogs.

Most of the time Meg can be found running between softball fields, hockey rinks, band concerts, and various sports lessons with the kids. Meg is an avid reader and will read any book from any genre.

Truth be told, she is a ridiculous fan of Supernatural (yes, the show.)

In February 2016, Meg received an award from the readers of the DeSoto Times Tribune naming her as DeSoto County Mississippi's Best Author 2015.

A Place to Stand is Meg's first book which was written during NaNoWriMo 2013 and released July 2014. It is available on Amazon for purchase as a print book or e-book.

Connect with Meg on social media:

- Facebook: Author Meg Farrell
- Twitter: @authorMFarrell
- Instagram: @authormfarrell
- Tumblr: FarrellWrites

Contact Meg for speaking engagements or conference appearances at FarrellWrites@gmail.com .

Love an indie author? Leave a review! (Goodreads and Amazon)